FIDDLEFOOT JONES
of the North Woods

FIDDLEFOOT

JONES

of the North Woods

by Philip D. Jordan

ILLUSTRATED BY HANS HELWEG

New York, The Vanguard Press

for five Jordans
Martha
Sandy Q.
Kip
Jeff
Jon
in memory of
their Grandfathers

Contents

About Fiddlefoot Jones

There never was such a man as Fiddlefoot Jones.

I know because he was my friend, and I heard him tell stories by the hour. I always called him Plum Nelly Jones, although a lot of his friends liked Fiddlefoot better. He'd come by each name honestly enough. Folks in Minnesota's north country got to calling him "Plum Nelly" for a very good reason. Whenever he started on a trip—and he was a great traveler, as you will see—he always said he was going "plum out of the state and nea'ly out of the country." He said this so much that his friends, my father among them, called him Plum Nelly. I called him Plum Nelly also, just as Kit and Sandy do in this book. By the time I knew him he was along in life and most of his adventures were over, but he was still as compact and strong as a much younger man. He looked just like the Plum Nelly Jones who spun yarns for the Duncan boys.

And Plum Nelly certainly had more stories in him than most any other man I ever knew—he most certainly did. For one thing, he was a good deal of a fiddlefoot, and this is how he earned the name of Fiddlefoot Jones. A fiddlefoot, you known, is a person who isn't content to stay in one place very long. A fiddlefoot has an itching foot, and an itching foot wants to hit the trail, follow the rivers, push a canoe into hidden lakes. A fiddlefoot is willing to work at almost anything, providing it isn't the same kind of job he's worked at before. Plum Nelly was a sure-enough fiddlefoot, and it's no wonder folks got to calling him Fiddlefoot Jones.

When he was about fourteen, Plum Nelly hired out as a cook's helper in a lumber camp up on the Big Fork River. He passed around the pancakes in the morning and washed dishes. He saw the logs cut that went to Rat Portage in Canada. A few seasons later he labored as an axman and teamster and company clerk in camps along Beef Slough and Pelican River and Thief River. He logged the Bow String and Bug Creek. But he never held any one job for long.

He fiddlefooted into the wheat fields of North Dakota, where he brought in the harvest; he tried cowboying once, but horses never liked him, and he cared less for them; he snooped around Colorado's Frying Pan River and Dirty Woman Creek; he even took a turn as a roustabout on a Missouri steamboat. He sailed the Great Lakes. Once he got himself named a deputy sheriff, but Plum Nelly told my father, who told me, that he couldn't stand wearing a star. He handed it in the day after they pinned it on him and took off to work for a spell in a livery stable even though he didn't like horses. "You can depend on oxen, but not horses," he told my father.

Plum Nelly was a grown-up man before he ever set foot in a regular school with books and blackboards and pot-bellied stoves to warm pupils' rears in winter. He got his learning during the cold months and did odd jobs in the summer. There wasn't much he couldn't do—he worked as a blacksmith, he mended harness, he tried surveying. He ran a trap line even when he was in school. He was a fairly competent carpenter and a tolerable stonemason. He could lay a line of pipe and solder a tight joint. The first time I ever saw him he said, "Bub, there isn't anything I can't do or haven't tried to do." I think he was right.

Plum Nelly, at some time or other in his life, taught school. He only spoke about being a schoolmaster once or twice, but my father met a man around Bismarck, North Dakota, who said he had been to school to Plum Nelly and that he was a fine teacher. "He never laid a strap to me once," the man told Father. I know he liked books and became a great reader. He owned lots of books when I first visited his cabin. They were piled on shelves over his bunk, and he kept more in the kitchen, close to his rocking chair.

It was funny sometimes to hear Plum Nelly talk—one minute he sounded like a backwoodsman and in the next breath he put out sentences better than a lot of preachers can. All this helped make him the wonderful storyteller he was—this, and the experiences he'd had and the tales he had picked up from all kinds of folks—Indians and French Canadians and hunters and boatmen and cowboys and farmers and deckhands on a Missouri River steamboat. And he could make up stories about anything.

But, you know, these were *real* stories because he put real things into them: the way a mallard duck falls when shot hits it, the smell of sweet fern, the color of the sky at false dawn. He knew the ways and habits of living things, and he understood and respected the forest animals and the birds of the sky. It was Plum Nelly who first showed me a sunfish nest with the parent hovering over and fanning the eggs with its tail. My father always said that Plum Nelly, when he wanted to, could think like an animal or a bird or a fish. He was that smart in nature's ways.

Best of all, Plum Nelly was a laughing man. I think, perhaps, he had learned that the best way to take life is not to take it too seriously. This is why many of his stories carried such a broad streak of exaggeration and humor. "There's not enough fun in the world," he told me the last time I saw him. "To laugh is to live." Again, I think he was right. And he was a simple man with a love of plain things. His one great weakness was clothes—gaudy, bright-colored outfits loud enough to scare even a loud-dresser. I think Plum Nelly formed this taste when he was younger and found himself so very poor. He once told me that he had saved for six months to buy a broad-brimmed Western hat, the kind cowpunchers wear even today.

And it can't be denied that he was a play actor. Nothing

tickled him more than to set up situations and make them come to a happy ending. His imagination was boundless, even when he stopped his fiddlefooting around and settled down as a guide in northern Minnesota. The secret panel you will read about in this book actually did keep a real boy busy and excited on a short autumn visit to Plum Nelly's cabin on the shores of Woman Lake. I was that boy. Plum Nelly built the secret panel, carved the clue on its door, and wrote out all the hints and hid all the gifts. I found them just the way Kit and Sandy did. And Yellow Dog Dingo was a real dog, and he really met up with a skunk, and we really gave him a bath in tomato juice!

I'll tell you another secret. Plum Nelly made me a backwoods colonel when I was the age of freckle-faced Kit. The birch roll he gave me then is tattered and worn now, and its sky-blue ribbons are faded, but I still remember the excitement of receiving it. There was an honest-to-goodness cave on Plum Nelly's land, and in it he found what Sandy did—but I won't spoil the story by telling you what the treasure was.

Plum Nelly is gone now, but his old place on Broadwater Bay still stands, and deer still roam the woods nearby, and loons teach their young to swim and laugh and cry. The Woodtick Trail still abounds with ruffed grouse, and the snowshoe rabbits scurry through windfalls as they always have. In Woman Lake bass plop after fat frogs in the reed beds off Pew's Point, and walleyed pike are just as hungry for red lures as they were when Plum Nelly fed them his red flannels.

Lyman and Ethel Newlin live now where Plum Nelly had his cabin, and sometimes I think Lyman knows almost as much as Plum Nelly about the forest and the lakes and their creatures. He and I have told Plum Nelly's yarns over and over again. He helped me remember some of them.

There were others who encouraged me to write down Plum Nelly's tales, even though they never knew him as I did. Julius Nolte and Louise P. Olsen, of Minneapolis, were mighty helpful, as was Emma L. Brock of St. Paul. Carl Carmer liked the stories. The Louis W. and Maud Hill Family Foundation in St. Paul generously gave me a grant, so that I could devote a summer to bringing these yarns together. I am grateful, indeed, to the Foundation's director, A. A. Heckman, for his interest, and to the Folk Arts Foundation of America, Inc., for the role it played.

To my friend Moritz Jagendorf goes a special tribute. A wonderfully skilled storyteller, he has consistently demonstrated his interest in Plum Nelly, has lent a hand on innumerable occasions, has always been loyal and steadfast.

Most of all, however, Plum Nelly Jones himself made this book. These are his stories, and I have only set them down as I remember his telling them.

P.D.J.

FIDDLEFOOT JONES
of the North Woods

1 *Operation Plum Nelly*

Kit, his freckled face all puckered in thought, went over the list in his hand for the umpty-umpth time.

"Glass trolling rod?" he asked.

"Yup," answered Sandy, Kit's younger brother, who was riding in the front seat with Mr. Duncan.

"Canned onion flakes for soup?" Kit continued.

"Of course!"

Kit checked onions off his list. "What about long under- wear? Mother said we'd sure need it."

"Yup," said Sandy again. "It's in the duffel bag."

"Dad's new minnow bucket? Didja put that in?"

Sandy nodded.

"And Yellow Dog Dingo's biscuits?" Hearing his name, Dingo waved his tail. He was a sad-eyed, floppy-eared hound with a lolling tongue the size of a slice of breakfast ham.

With a stubby pencil, Kit neatly crossed out dog biscuits. "Next is Dad's case of shotgun shells. Didja—"

"For Pete's sake," said Sandy, "clam up! We've got everything." He turned to his father. "Haven't we, Dad?"

"If we haven't, it's too late now. We're four hundred miles from home, and I'm not going back for anything." Mr. Duncan stepped on the gas. "Put that list away, Kit, and enjoy yourself. We're not too far from Plum Nelly's."

Since early morning the Duncan car, loaded with wilderness equipment, had followed the highway north—from rolling prairie land, through old lumbering regions, and now into the lake country, where towns were few and the road passed water of deepest blue and wound through stands of pines so tall their tops seemed to touch sky.

To Kit and Sandy the ride was endless. They had planned this trip for months, ever since they learned their school would be closed so their teachers could go to a convention. Mr. Duncan, who always went hunting this time of year, promised he'd take the boys with him to visit Plum Nelly. It was lucky indeed that a school vacation came at exactly the same time as their father's hunting trip.

For some silly reason Plum Nelly's camp on Broadwater Bay seemed farther away, now that they were actually getting near it, than when Mr. Duncan had first mentioned the trip. Perhaps this was because the boys had been so busy getting ready they had given small thought to time and so time had passed swiftly. With cash from his paper route, Kit had bought a beautiful level-winding reel. And Sandy had made enough money raking leaves to purchase a spanking new windbreaker. Days before zero hour, the boys' room was a litter of rods and tackle boxes and packs and duffel bags. "That stuff," Mrs. Duncan called it.

This was the boys' first trip to the north woods. They had planned for it as carefully as if charting the first space flight to the moon. Kit made dozens of lists. When the lads weren't sorting their own gear, they watched Mr. Duncan's preparations. They saw their father slide oil-soaked cleaning patches through his shotguns—the heavy twelve-gauge and the smaller double-barreled .410. They packed and repacked boots, mackinaws, and woolen stockings with crimson tops until all fitted into the smallest space.

Kit, bursting with importance, told his Scout troop he was going to live in a log cabin with an old-time lumberjack; and Sandy, not to be outdone, told anybody who would listen that he was going to sleep in a real bunk and, if the weather got too cold, he had a *gen-u-ine* sleeping bag to crawl into. Plum Nelly Jones, Sandy said, knew more about hunting and fishing than any man alive—why, he was a greater woodsman than Daniel Boone!

"Dad, when are we going to get there?" Kit spoke from the back seat he shared with Yellow Dog Dingo. His voice came out of a pile of gun cases, metal shell boxes, and blanket rolls. It was hard for him to look out, too, for Dingo's wet nose had smeared the car windows. When Mr. Duncan didn't answer, Kit yanked Sandy's ear. "Hey you!" he cried.

"What do you want?" Sandy turned to see Kit better.

"When are we going to get there? I'm getting tired, aren't you, Sandy?"

"Pretty soon now, I guess. No, I'm not tired—I'm starved."

Kit was disgusted. "You're always hungry. Mother says she can never fill you up." He looked at his wrist watch. "Why, we only ate two hours ago. And what did you have? You gobbled two hamburgers, a malted milk, and a piece of pie with ice cream. Even you can't be that hungry!"

"Why can't I?" said Sandy.

Kit sighed. "I guess *you* can." He spoke to his father. "Say, Dad, how far is it now? You said maybe we'd get to Broadwater in time for supper, and it's getting dark."

"Sit tight, son." Mr. Duncan swung the car past a truck loaded with timber. "Questions won't make the trip shorter or the car faster. If nothing happens, we'll be at Broadwater in half an hour. Look at the color on that maple!"

This was autumn, when the weather crisped and leaves turned color to make the woods a blaze of browns, yellows, and crimsons. This was October, when giant geese came honking down from Canada, and mallards, teal, bluebills, and redheads, silent as ghosts, coasted into the narrows and shallows of Broadwater Bay. This was the season when ruffed grouse with their stand-out collars stuffed themselves with berries and leaves, and when deer began thinking about raising families. But, best of all, this was the time when Plum Nelly had leisure to entertain the Duncans.

"Pop," asked Sandy, "will Mr. Plum Nelly be waiting for us—will he meet us at camp?"

"I think so," smiled his father. "He'll want to tell you

about his adventures. He's a great storyteller. He can talk pretty as a schoolbook one minute and rough as a back-woodsman the next."

"I know," chimed in Kit, who liked to talk. "Plum Nelly's the best storyteller in Minnesota—maybe in the whole world. Will he tell us about the woods' monkeys?"

Mr. Duncan laughed. "Oh, he'll tell you all the tales you want. Plum Nelly's got all the secrets of the wilderness. He's lived up here man and boy for more than fifty years. He knows where the deer feed and where the bears live. Old Plum Nelly can smell out the right place to set a trap or drop a fishline. I never saw such a man. Sometimes I think he's part beaver. Why, one time he—"

"But are you sure he's going to be there?" interrupted Sandy impatiently.

"Sure, I'm sure," answered his father. "Now, you boys hang on to your seats and watch Dingo. From here on the road is mighty rough."

He swung the car off the pavement into a gravel road, a lane that narrowed and was squeezed together by dense underbrush. A patch of swamp, guarded by cattails in brown helmets, went by. Sandy pointed out a hay meadow. Mr. Duncan said hay meadows were good places to see deer when they fed at dusk.

Kit craned his neck, pushing Yellow Dog Dingo away from the window. "I don't see any deer."

"Stupid," yelled Sandy. "It's too late to see 'em. It's past dusk."

"I'm not either stupid." Kit turned on his brother. "I guess I know it's too late—I just said I didn't see any. Didn't I, Pop?"

"No, you're not stupid, Kit, and neither are you, Sandy. But it isn't a good thing to lose your temper in the woods."

A left-hand turn, marked by a forlorn tar-paper shanty, took the Duncans' automobile into a still narrower road, a winding, rutty cutoff that made wheels skip and spin and bounced boys and dog into the air. "We're on the Wood-tick Trail," cautioned Mr. Duncan. "Hang on." The Wood-tick Trail went uphill and down, so that the engine groaned in second gear one minute and raced against the brake the next. Then came a stretch of sand, a mud hole, and a quarter mile of rocks. In the back seat, Kit bumped up and down like a jumping jack. *Thump,* and Kit was up; *thump,* and he was down! A long-necked crane, balancing on one leg and looking for all the world like a boy on stilts, spread its ridiculous wings and flapped away.

Then Sandy spied the arrow. "Lookit!" he cried. "There's a road sign." It was rough-hacked from an old board, and swayed from a rotting post. Its tip pointed straight ahead. Kit scrambled out as Mr. Duncan stopped the car and centered his flashlight on crude letters.

"What does it say, son?" Mr. Duncan leaned out of the car.

"It says, 'Plum Nelly Jones—Broadwater Bay ¼ mile,' " called Kit, snapping off the light. He stumbled back into the car. "Move over, Yellow Dog Dingo, and give me some room. There, that's better."

"I thought this was right," muttered Mr. Duncan, shifting gears, "but I haven't been up here in a long time and the country looks different this time of day."

Minutes later the Duncans rattled across corduroy planking, made a half circle, and stopped in front of a log building. Kit and Sandy never had seen such a cabin. It stood right in the center of a clump of Christmas trees, firs and spruces whose dark branches contrasted with the high polish of the cabin's varnished logs. And the house was bigger —much bigger—than the boys had ever dreamed. It was square and solid, with a huge stone fireplace at one end and a little front stoop with birch railings at the other. A kerosene lamp with a bright blue shade burned bright in the front window. The boys smelled wood smoke, the tantalizing sweet-sour odor so common in the north country. Dingo lifted his long nose and sniffed.

"Plum Nelly's home, all right." Mr. Duncan slid stiffly from under the wheel. "Let's go in and say hello. We'll unpack later."

As he spoke, the cabin door banged back. Framed in the light stood a spry little man with a thin fuzz of reddish-brown hair spread over his head, and dark brown eyes that laughed. He might have been forty or sixty or seventy or even older. His cheeks were high and weathered to the color of russet leather. A stubby pipe was held tight in his teeth.

"Great guns and pickled pigs' feet!" chirped Plum Nelly. "Don't stand there! Come in, come in!"

The Duncans stepped into their first adventure.

2 *"If You Know A from Z"*

Kit was disappointed with Plum Nelly.

"Why, he isn't big at all," he whispered to Sandy when Plum Nelly was outside helping unload.

Kit had expected a giant with mighty shoulders and barrel chest, a man whose muscle-corded legs wouldn't buckle under the weight of a canoe or bend under a hundred pounds or more of green hides. But Plum Nelly was no big man at all. He was slight, with narrow shoulders that tapered to even narrower hips. He slendered again from hips to feet. He wore buckskin moccasins that at first glance looked frail enough for dancing and not rugged enough to travel a trail. Why, thought Sandy, he's built like a slim runner.

"Didn't Dad say Plum Nelly was one of the strongest men he ever knew?" Sandy said to Kit. "His hands aren't wide enough to go round a—"

"S-s-sh," hissed Kit. "Here they come."

"Well, lads, shuck off those clothes because grub'll be ready in a jiffy." Plum Nelly didn't give the boys time to answer. "You're hungry, I suppose. Great guns and pickled pigs' feet! We'll feed you so you won't look so dang peaked, put you to bed, and tomorrow fix you up with warm duds. Kit, pull the table over in front of the fire. Sandy, you scatter some eatin' tools around. Now git goin'—the knives and spoons are in the cupboard drawer." He grinned at Mr. Duncan. "John, we'll make woodsmen out of these boys of yours if it takes a year with two winters."

Kit kept his eyes peeled as he helped Sandy set the table. The table was handmade, as was a pine gun rack that filled a corner by the roaring fire. Gay-colored curtains were fashioned from flour sacks and stitched with nylon fishline. The floor was laid with wide boards, scrubbed and polished to reflect dancing points of light from lamp and fireplace. But what attracted Kit most, so that he could scarcely tend to his table-setting, was a small door, a panel set cunningly into the rough native stones of the fireplace. Only about five inches square, the door was fastened with hasp and padlock. Kit nudged Sandy and pointed to it. "There's something written on it. Go see what it says."

Sandy sauntered carelessly to the fireplace, spreading

his hands toward the heat. Plum Nelly stirred a pot simmering on the stove, and Mr. Duncan, busy in the bunkroom, was spreading blankets on a doubledecker. Sandy edged closer to the mysterious panel. The writing on the tiny door had been burned deep into the strong wood, and the panel itself was trimmed with brass, the way a ship's treasure box in pirate days was bound. A step nearer, and Sandy, standing a little on tiptoe, made out the legend. His eyes popped and his breath went "whoosh!" Then Plum Nelly turned around, a steaming bowl in each hand.

"Soup's on. Come and get it or I'll throw it away!"

Mr. Duncan laughed. "This one of your famous stews, Plum Nelly? The kind you sop in?" He crumbled black bread into the bowl. "Boys, here's a whole meal in one dish. Forget what your mother says about dunking at home—you're in the woods now and"—Mr. Duncan's voice became deeply official—"and I hereby declare that dunking is good manners."

The soup, thick and heavy, steamed with a delicious odor. As he spooned it to his lips, Kit wondered what the panel said, but he was afraid to ask Sandy in front of Plum Nelly. He decided to wait until bedtime. That was when he and Sandy had most of their private talks anyhow. He finished his bowl, feeling that he could never eat another bite.

"That's good." He wiped his mouth, crushing a paper napkin and dropping it into the empty bowl, the way Plum Nelly did. "What was in the stew, Plum Nelly?"

Plum Nelly scraped back his chair, kindled a blackened brier pipe, and puffed contentedly. "A full stomach is one of the first laws of the woods," he said. "Just like never pointing a gun at anything you don't expect to kill." He scratched another match. "What's in my soup, you say, Kit? Why, the usual victuals, I guess—onions and potatoes and rabbit and odds and ends of grouse and a couple of squirrels I shot this morning and some carrots and—oh yes, agropelter."

"Agro—what, Plum Nelly?" Sandy wasn't sure he had heard right. The soup had warmed him and made him drowsy. Yellow Dog Dingo lifted his head, hauled himself to his feet, and then, as if all this was too much effort, collapsed on the floor, tucking his tail under his chin and going to sleep.

"Goodness me," said Plum Nelly, looking at Sandy as if he had never seen him before and wasn't quite sure what peculiar kind of animal he was. "Why, goodness me. Do you mean to sit there and tell me you don't know what kind of a critter an agropelter is?" Plum Nelly twisted in his chair to point his pipe at Mr. Duncan. "John, haven't you told these lads about agropelters?"

When Mr. Duncan shook his head, Kit couldn't stand it any longer. "What *is* an agropelter, Plum Nelly?" he blurted, then suddenly felt ashamed that he had forgotten himself.

"I guess you lads are really tenderfeet." Plum Nelly sounded serious, but his brown eyes twinkled and a half smile went round the pipe stem. "Listen now, and I'll tell you." He leaned back in the chair, legs crossed, one moccasin dangling from a foot.

"A long time ago—I don't really know how far back, but it was before I was a boy—a trapper by the name of Pierre came pushing into this north country. Pierre was a mighty hunter, there's no doubt of that. The Chippewa Indians, who used to live just about where this cabin stands, said Pierre's winter kill was bigger than any other trapper in the forest. And Pierre was as good a shot as he was a snaremaker. He had an old trade gun that kicked him backwards nigh half a mile every time flint sparked powder. But Pierre's musket could really kill. He shot ducks flying so high in the sky he had to use salted bullets, so the ducks wouldn't spoil during their long fall to ground." Sandy giggled.

"Pierre," continued Plum Nelly, pretending not to notice, "Pierre was a dandy all done up in fringed buckskin with scarlet sash around his middle and a crimson cap shaped like an overgrown acorn atop his head. And he was always singin'. You'd think he'd scare game away with that bull voice of his, but it never worked that way. I don't know why. It was the singin' that got him into trouble, you might say. Anyway, it was his habit of singin' that found the agropelters.

"One day Pierre took his gun and powder flask, intending to shoot him some squirrel for stew, just the way I did this morning when I was fixin' to make supper tonight for you boys. He started down Woodtick Trail singin' at the top of his lungs and searching treetops for red squirrels —reds have better flavor than gray squirrels. He hadn't gone very far before he noticed that Mr. Squirrel wasn't chattering and talking the way he usually did. Squirrels can be like old women when they want to—gossipy. 'Umph,' said Pierre, 'thees is funny.' Right then, peeking behind the pinkish bark of a Norway pine, he glimpsed a furry face. At first Pierre thought it was a new kind of squirrel."

"What was it?" Kit interrupted.

"Kit!" cautioned his father; and Kit kept still.

"As I was saying," Plum Nelly continued, "Pierre saw this furry face way up in the top of a pine. He lifted his gun, but every time he aimed, the face ran around to the other side of the tree. Before he knew it, Pierre was running circles around the trunk. Every time he was on one side, the animal was making faces at him from the other. Pierre got so tired he had to sit down to rest. While he rested, he sang. Pretty soon he noticed the furry face was a little closer, so he sang some more. And the longer the song went on, the closer came the animal. Closer, and closer, and closer, until Pierre's hand shot out and caught it!

"It had a long nose, a mouth with sharp teeth, fuzzy ears, and a long tail, like a monkey's. But it was the hands that really surprised Pierre. They had four fingers and a jointed thumb, just like mine." Plum Nelly wiggled his fingers. "And it was smaller than a squirrel, small enough for Pierre to tuck in the pocket of his hunting shirt. It stayed there, its bright eyes peeking out under the flap, all the way back to Pierre's cabin and didn't seem the least surprised or frightened. 'Wat you t'ink of dat?' said Pierre. 'He wan leetle agropelter.' "

"Pierre didn't put him in the stew, did he?" cried Sandy, so horrified he forgot the secret panel.

Plum Nelly laughed. "No, Pierre kept him."

"What did Pierre want with a thing like that?" asked Kit.

"First off," answered Plum Nelly, "Pierre couldn't figure out just what to do with the critter. He tamed easy
enough, so that in a week or so he was following Pierre
around like Yellow Dog Dingo follows you, Kit. Then one
Saturday afternoon Pierre decided he'd paddle over to
Cut Foot Sioux to the dance, thinking it'd been a long
time since he'd heard the fiddle scrape and the callers
shout 'Swing yer partners, everybody!' So he got out his
fancy clothes: the blue coat with brass buttons, his best
pantaloons, and his dancin' shoes—soft leather they were,
with little jingly bells sewed around the uppers. But he
couldn't find a pair of stockings that didn't have a hole in
them. Before he could go, Pierre had to mend a pair. The
agropelter, his sharp eyes missing nothing, watched Pierre
thread the needle, pull the hole together, and hurry
from the cabin. Pierre never wanted to keep girls waiting.

"Early next morning when Pierre came home the agropelter, all curled up in a sleepy knot with his tail over
his face to keep him warm, didn't even wake up, and this
was unusual, for usually the tiny creature hopped up and
down with pleasure and squeaked a long string of wel-
comes. Pierre couldn't understand it. Then he looked
around. On the table lay a pile of neatly darned socks,
each hole closed with careful stitches and every stocking
mated as to color—the blue with the blue, the red with the
red, and the black for Sunday Mass with the black. The
agropelter had done it all. After that Pierre called his pet
'Needle Eye.'" Plum Nelly glanced at the dying fire. "I
better put a night log on."

"But is that all?" wailed Sandy. "What happened to

Needle Eye, and why did you put such a nice animal like him in the soup tonight?"

"Oh! I forgot," said Plum Nelly, settling back. He tickled Yellow Dog Dingo's long nose, so that the hound grumbled deep in his chest and rolled over, all four feet in the air and his tail beating a lazy tattoo on the floor. "No, that isn't all, Sandy, but I thought maybe you were sleepy, like Dingo here."

"Of course I'm not sleepy. Plum Nelly, we didn't eat Needle Eye tonight, did we?" Sandy appealed to his father. "Did we, Dad?"

"No," said his father.

"Pierre and Needle Eye got along beautifully together for a good many years," said Plum Nelly. Kit and Sandy drew big sighs of relief. "Needle Eye became such an excellent mender that his fame spread all over Cass County. At first he didn't have too much to do, because not many people lived around here, but pretty soon the lumberjacks came piling in—the cutters and choppers and trimmers and the cooks and clerks and wagon drivers. Those Swedes and Norwegians couldn't mend stockings for sour apples, if you know what I mean. Pretty soon they were bringing all their darning to Needle Eye, and that little fellow used his eyes so much Pierre had to go to town and get a pair of spectacles for him.

"After about a year, Needle Eye slipped from Pierre's cabin one Monday night and was gone a week. He came back with four other agropelters and, bless me, if he didn't teach every single one of them to darn. Then he sent 'em around to the logging camps. When more lumberjacks came into the woods and more socks were to be mended, the four recruited new agropelters, until, when lumbering was at its peak up here, there were 1,286 agropelters working as tailors, sitting cross-legged on benches and sewing and stitching and biting off thread with their sharp little teeth.

"All of a sudden, the faithful tailors quit work and disappeared, leaving their scissors and thimbles and a mound of unfinished mending. Oh, the lumber companies advertised for them and offered rewards, and camp bosses sent search parties through the woods, but nobody found a single agropelter. Even Needle Eye deserted Pierre, running off without a good-by or word of appreciation for the good home Pierre had given him. Ungrateful little wretch! Some folks say the agropelters just grew tired of working and lit out for Canada; I dunno—others think Needle Eye and his friends couldn't stand to see the big trees fall and the woods disappear. After that, lumberjacks mended their own socks."

"But Plum Nelly," protested Kit, his face puckered with thought and the freckles on his nose standing out like question marks, "if all the agropelters disappeared, how did you cook one in our stew tonight?"

"Listen, boys." Plum Nelly stirred Yellow Dog Dingo with his toe. "Today in the woods we use 'agropelter' to mean something that isn't—something that's not present. Agropelter means *a lot of nothing!*" Plum Nelly grinned briefly. "If you go fishing and don't catch a fish, what do you do? You come home and say, 'Never had better luck in my life—caught my limit of agropelters!' The good sport never whines when his stringer or game pocket is empty. That's why I always add agropelter meat to my stews; it gives them added flavor and makes my guests remember that sportsmanship comes first in this cabin! Off to bed now; we've got things to do in the morning!"

Minutes later, Kit, from the snugness of the top bunk, looked down at Sandy.

"Sandy," he whispered, "are you asleep?"

"Not yet," mumbled Sandy.

"What did the secret panel say?"

"It said,"—Sandy crinkled his brow in an effort to remember exactly the astonishing words burned on the panel—"it said:

> *If you know A from Z and 1 from 3*
> *Twist right or left to set me free.*"

Kit almost fell out of the bunk. "You're foolin', Sandy!"

"No, I'm not," said Sandy stoutly. "And, Kit—"

"Yup?"

"Kit, there was a—" Sandy gulped—"there was a skull and crossbones on it, too!"

3 *How Plum Nelly's Red Flannels Caught Pike*

Next morning Kit heard sausage sizzling and smelled the good, clean odor of wood smoke. A coffee mill clattered and an oven door slammed. Sandy still slept, one arm thrown across his face and the other dangling from the bunk. Kit was just ready to throw off his blankets when he heard voices from the kitchen.

"I tell you, John," Plum Nelly was saying, "those boys will want to be up and doing today. They aren't goin' to be content sitting around and resting. Hand me that fork, will you; this sausage needs turnin'."

"I know it," the boys' father answered. "But I don't want to tire 'em out the first day we're here. They had a long trip yesterday, and they're not going to be in any shape to go gallivanting through the woods like a jack-pine savage."

Kit slipped quietly from bed. The floor chilled his bare feet, and goose pimples climbed his legs.

Plum Nelly's voice came again. "Who says I'm goin' to gallivant through the woods?" He tramped to the window. He had changed from the soft moccasins of the night before to laced boots. "I'm goin' to take Kit and Sandy fly-fishin' for crappie," he grumbled, as if daring Mr. Duncan to say "no." "That ain't goin' to hurt 'em none. While we're gone, you take your double-barrel out on the Point. Bring back a mess of grouse for dinner. They'll be peckin' gravel on that old lumber road this morning."

Plum Nelly spied Kit. "What you doin', boy, in naked feet? Is Sandy up? Get your clothes on and come to break-fast. We're goin' fishin' this morning, if I can get your old man out of my hair. Is he always this much bother at home, Kit?" Plum Nelly was still talking, asking questions, and answering himself while Kit excitedly threw on his clothes—long underwear, wool trousers, heavy shirt, and shoes with crepe soles that wouldn't slip in a boat. Sandy was ready when Kit was, and the boys, after washing in a tin basin and slicking down their hair, entered the kitchen.

"Gee, that smells good," said Sandy. "I could eat a bear."

"Haven't got bear this mornin'," said Plum Nelly, filling plates. "If you can make out on sausage and eggs and fried mush and hot biscuits, okay. If you gotta have bear, you'll have to board someplace else."

Sandy grinned. "I'll try your food first." He tucked a napkin under his chin and pulled the platter toward him. "Mother says I eat anything."

"And at any time," put in his father.

"I'd be ashamed to eat as much as he does," said Kit, helping himself to another egg, sunny side up.

"Who's taking seconds right now?" cried Sandy.

"Eat all you want, both of you," smiled Plum Nelly. "Everybody's hungry up here, and you'd better fill up because we've got work to do."

Kit didn't have time to talk to Sandy alone until after breakfast, when the dishes were washed, bunks made, and the floor swept. Their first chance came when Plum Nelly sent them for slabs to fill the wood box. Walking back from the slab pile, their arms filled, Kit turned to Sandy.

"Sandy, what did the secret panel say again? Plum Nelly kept me so busy I didn't get time to look."

Sandy stumbled, and a piece of wood tumbled from the load, setting Yellow Dog Dingo to chasing it and barking. "Stop it, Dingo!" Sandy staggered on with the load. "It said:

> *If you know A from Z and 1 from 3*
> *Twist right or left to set me free.*"

"What's that?" A loud voice boomed behind them, and there was Plum Nelly, come to see if he could lend a hand. Sandy's armful of chunks flew in every direction. The boy turned his scarlet face to the guide. "You boys come into the house with me."

"Now, then," said Plum Nelly a few minutes later, when the slabs were dumped into the box behind the stove, "what's all this about A and Z and one and three? You been monkeying with my treasure box?"

Kit fidgeted and Sandy couldn't seem to say anything, although his mouth opened and shut and a lump in his throat kept gulping up and down. Kit's eyes bulged. He and Sandy just stood, foolish-like, wishing they'd never seen the little door set so cunningly in the fireplace. Even Yellow Dog Dingo dropped his tail.

"Well?" prompted Plum Nelly, not at all grim the way his voice sounded, but appearing pleased with himself.

Sandy looked at Kit, and Kit looked at Sandy. They both looked at Dingo, but he had disappeared under the table, his tawny head flat on the floor and his sad brown eyes asking: *Now, what did you want to meddle with that old panel for?*

Suddenly Plum Nelly, whose face had been twitching suspiciously all the time, smiled—a smile that twinkled his eyes and brought roars of laughter from him. He laughed so hard tears streamed down his cheeks and he had to wipe them away with a red handkerchief. When Plum Nelly smiled, the boys smiled too, and soon they were chortling as hard as Plum Nelly, although they didn't quite know why.

"And I thought you hadn't seen it," sputtered Plum Nelly, wiping his eyes again. Then he became serious. "You know, fellows, the combination on that door is a hard one to work, but—" he paused—"but there's treasure inside for anyone who can do it."

"Really, Plum Nelly?" said Kit. "You're not fooling?"
"You're not fooling?" echoed Sandy, looking at Plum Nelly doubtfully.

"Of course I'm not fooling." Plum Nelly acted indignant. "Anybody who can open the door gets the treasure. That's a promise!"

"Then I'm going to work on it right now," shouted Kit, running toward the fireplace.

"Wait a minute!" The boys stopped at Plum Nelly's command. "We're goin' fishin' now. Treasure hunting is for later, anyhow."

Plum Nelly's dock, fashioned from oil drums to which planks were lashed, swayed gently with an offshore wind. Made in the shape of a T, it had a crossbar some forty feet from shore. Such an arrangement, Plum Nelly pointed out, permitted boats to dock on three sides. At the far end, the Stars and Stripes fluttered from a tall pole. Two boats were moored to the dock, a wooden rowboat painted white with a green strip on the gunnel, and an aluminum boat that shone in the morning sun. On the bow of each boat was painted the figure 4.

"What's the four for?" said Sandy, puzzled.

Plum Nelly looked up from the outboard motor he was clamping to the aluminum boat's stern. "All boats in the north country are inspected by the State Board of Health," he explained, "and the seating capacity of each boat is painted on the bow. It's against the law to overload a boat. My boats are safe for four persons and no more. The man who overloads a boat doesn't care if he lives or drowns." Plum Nelly twisted the last clamp tightly. "That reminds me," he continued, "did you fellows bring life preservers?"

"No," said Kit. "Dad didn't say a thing about them."

"Then run up to the boathouse and fetch three of 'em —not the cushions, mind you, but the kind that go on like a jacket. There's no sense in going out in a boat without a life jacket."

The boathouse was a fascinating place. A minnow tank filled one end, and the other was shelved. Landing nets, gaff hooks, minnow buckets of canvas and metal, boxes of trolling spoons and brightly feathered spinners, bell sinkers and snap-on sinkers—all these were arranged as neatly as in a store. When Kit returned with the life jackets, Sandy and Plum Nelly had stowed their gear in the boat and were ready to push off. With a jerk of the starting string, the motor boomed into life.

"We're off," cried Plum Nelly, making a wide circle and setting a course for Bear Island, a rocky, wild-looking place with a few sickly stands of pine and scrub oak. Then suddenly he cut the engine. "You get a good view of my place from here," he said, pointing. "There's my cabin, and off to the right is the icehouse. That's where you picked up the slabwood this morning. This way from the ice-house is my barn—it's near fifty years old, I reckon, but it's still sound enough to protect my jeep in winter. Other times, I let 'er stand out. Now look, this way is north and that's south; over here is east, and there's west. Got it straight, Kit?"

"I . . . I guess so," said Kit a little doubtfully.

"Well, you better if you don't want to get lost. A fellow can lose himself mighty easy, and it's no fun to be lost on a lake or spend a night in the woods because you don't know directions. You bring a compass?"

"No," chorused both boys.

"Didn't you now?" The boys thought Plum Nelly looked pleased, although at the moment they didn't understand why. "No use talkin' all day," added Plum Nelly quickly, and started up the motor once more.

Twenty minutes later they anchored on the lee side of Bear Island. Even in this sheltered cove the wind blew fitfully, sending uncomfortable gusts down necks and slapping water against the sides of the boat. A flock of geese honked across the sky. Across the bay a loon laughed in answer and quickly dived, embarrassed by the raucous echo flung from the island's cliff. Hearing the noise, a muskrat slipped from the roof of his half-submerged house and silently disappeared in the water.

"We'd better still-fish," said Plum Nelly, squinting at the wind. "There's too much breeze for fly casting. First fish wins a chocolate bar!"

Sandy tied a red and white bobber to his line, slipped a hook under a fat minnow's fin, and put his line overboard. Kit selected a cigar-shaped bobber, painted green with white stripes. The waves danced both bobbers away, pushing them toward shore. Plum Nelly, sprawled in the stern, used no bobber at all, preferring to let his bait sink almost to the bottom, where walleyed pike feed.

Sandy glued his eyes to the bobber, his hands clutching the pole as if at any moment a huge fish would rush away with both line and rod. Suddenly the gaily colored bobber dipped gracefully, half submerged, rose again, ran rapidly through the water, and sank. *Whew!* breathed Sandy to himself, *here's where I win the chocolate bar!* He yanked hard, feeling the strong surge of a fish. Kit turned in time to see Sandy yank again, a powerful pull. Then the line went slack. The fish was gone.

"Too bad," said Plum Nelly. "You pulled too hard—crappies have mighty tender mouths."

Sandy's face fell, and he threaded another minnow on his hook. He faced Kit, now smiling impishly. "I missed the crappie all right, but I got an agropelter!"

"That's the stuff," said Plum Nelly approvingly. "Now, that's a real sport talking. Did I ever tell you about the time I caught fish with my red underwear?"

"What?" said Kit.

"It happened years ago," said Plum Nelly, "before we had improved roads up here and when I was just about the only white man between here and Longville. I'd just finished cuttin' the logs for my cabin, and believe me, I was sick and tired of heaving them into place. Well, one morning I said, 'No more work for me.' I dug some worms back there where the icehouse is now, and netted a pail of shiner minnows at the mouth of the creek. I dropped a couple of June-bug spinners in one pocket and a handful of panfish poppers in the other. Those were the days when a feller could get all the fish he wanted in half an hour. I didn't know what was goin' to be bitin', but I figured I was ready for anything—worms for catfish and bluegills, shiners for walleyes and northerns, June bugs if the walleyes and northerns didn't like shiners, and poppers for crappie and sunfish.

"The weather was just like we're havin' today—wind in the right direction when I set out, but changing quick-like. It wasn't bad, just enough to stir up the lake a little. The waves, I reckon, were about like now. I anchored right in this cove, 'bout the exact spot where we're sitting. An old marsh rabbit with a stick in his mouth was—"

"I didn't know rabbits could swim," said Sandy, wide-eyed.

"We call muskrats marsh rabbits up here, because they taste like rabbits when they're cooked. Some say they're like chicken, but to me they are closer to rabbit." Plum Nelly pulled his bait up and let it drop back. "As I was sayin', an old marsh rabbit was swimming over yonder with a stick in his face, but he was the only living thing around. Now, you won't believe this, boys, but I fished for about two hours and never got a bite. Not a one, and I was beginning to get mad. I cast and I trolled and I still-fished—I tried every bait I had, live and artificial.

"Fish wouldn't bite on any of 'em. I put a worm and a minnow on a hook. That wasn't any good either. I baited my poppers with worms and didn't get a bite. Oh, there were fish in the cove. I could see them feeding in the shallows. Now and then one would jump. Kinda shake his tail at me, sassy-like."

"Didn't you give up?" Kit asked.

"Nope," said Plum Nelly. "I jest quit fishin' for a spell and thought. I looked through my pockets to see if I had anything to tease 'em with. Didn't have a thing. Then the sun came out, and I shucked out of my coat. It got hotter. I took my shirt off. I sat in the sun in my red flannels. By and by I happened to pick a loose thread off my flannels and toss it into the water. Wasn't even lookin' what I was doing. All of a sudden I hear a splash. Sounded like a whale tryin' to jump into the boat. I looks around and sees a walleye plungin' back into the water. He must've weighed ten or twelve pounds. *Oho,* thinks I, *he was after that red flannel!*

"So I takes my knife and cuts a piece from my under-shirt. Red as blood, it was. I slips the hook with the red flannel overboard. And I gives it a little flip. Bang! I've got a fish. I hauls him in, and he's a walleye. I figure he weighs close to fourteen pounds. So I strings him and cuts an-other piece from my underwear. Only this time I cuts a bigger piece. And I gets a bigger fish. The next patch I cut is bigger yet. I haul in a lunker—maybe eighteen pounds or more. I keep cuttin' and catchin' fish until pretty soon I'm sittin' there with no undershirt at all. So I starts on my pants, cuttin' chunks of red flannel and pullin' in wall-eyes every time I drops the baited hook in the lake. I use all the uppers of my pants and start on the right leg be-fore I notice. There I am with no shirt and half my britches cut off!

"My stringers are full, and pike are piled in the boat like cordwood. I say to myself that it's time to quit. But I don't. I try once more with a piece of red flannel a foot square on my hook. I no sooner get it in the water than a mouth comes up big as an alligator and sucks the last of my red flannels in. I've got the biggest pike in Broadwater Bay. I pull and he pulls. As fast as I reel in line, he takes it out. Pretty soon I notice the anchor rope standin' straight as a pointer's tail. Then it snaps! My boat starts out of the cove toward deep water. I don't know what to do."

"Couldn't you cut the line with your knife?" asked Kit.

"What for? I'd lose the fish that way."

"But what did you do?" Sandy forgot all about watch-ing his bobber.

"Where's your bobber, Sandy?" said Plum Nelly.

Sandy looked quickly. The float had disappeared, and line was running quietly from the reel. For a minute Sandy just looked. Then, carefully, without yanking, he reeled in, giving a little when the crappie tugged and taking in when the fish stopped pulling. "I've got him," he cried, lifting a beautiful silver and black fish into the boat. "And this time it's no agropelter! I win the chocolate bar!"

"Hurry up, Plum Nelly, and give him the prize," cried Kit.

"What's the hurry?" Plum Nelly said, handing Sandy the chocolate.

"I want to know what happened after the fish started pulling you across the lake," answered Kit.

"That monster was headin' for the deepest part of the lake, I could see that," Plum Nelly continued. "And I noticed that he kept sinking all the time. I begin to worry. I see the boat settle—inch by inch it sinks lower in the water. I heave the anchor out to lighten the load. Overboard goes the minnow pail, then the oars. The boat still sinks. Finally I toss all the fish back—the biggest I've ever caught. That hurt, I tell you. Even with all extra weight overboard, the gunnels are just above water. In another minute the boat will go down. I've never drowned before, and don't want to start now."

"Golly!" said Kit. "What did you do?"

"I grabbed my jackknife and cut a hole in the boat's bottom. That let the water drain out! And just then the huge fish broke my line and escaped. The boat righted itself, and I was saved."

"But how did you get home," asked Sandy, "without oars?"

Plum Nelly didn't seem to hear. "There I was," he said, "in the middle of the lake almost stark naked. I'd thrown away my fishing gear. And I'd lost the biggest walleye ever caught in Broadwater Bay. I paddled home with my hands." Plum Nelly was quiet for a minute. "You know, nobody ever would believe I caught record-breaking pike with red underwear for bait."

"Didn't you try again with red flannel?" asked Kit.

"I'd used up the last pair of colored drawers I had. 'Course, I bought another pair the next time I went to town, but that was six months later. By then the walleyes wouldn't touch the stuff, and from that day to this I've never caught anything on red flannel." Plum Nelly sighed, a long, drawn-out sigh. "You know," he added, "folks don't believe me when I tell this story. But lots of strange things happen in the woods."

Neither boy answered. Could it be that Plum Nelly was fooling them?

"Pull in your lines." Plum Nelly broke the silence. "The crappies aren't hitting. We might as well go home. Sandy's fish will make a meal for one." He started the motor.

Kit tied the boat to a dock post and helped Sandy and Plum Nelly unload. Then the boys ran for the cabin to open the secret panel. "What do you suppose is hidden there?" said Sandy.

4 Opening the Secret Panel

Kit and Sandy raced up the path from the lake to the cabin, flying feet kicking up showers of gravel. A hop-toad hurried out of the way. High on a branch a squirrel stopped gathering winter food long enough to chatter angrily.

"Here we are," puffed Kit, throwing open the door. He headed straight for the fireplace. The padlock still hung on the hasp, a lock that looked bright and new. It was designed like a safe's lock. A knob spun an arrow that pointed at figures and letters.

"Boy," breathed Sandy, peeling off his sweater, "that's not going to be easy to open." He took the padlock from Kit and twisted the knob. "Which way do we turn it?"

"I wish I knew," said Kit. He grabbed the lock from his brother. "Give it to me."

"I want to try first."

"We'll take turns," Kit said, still turning the arrow. "You can be first, if you want to, but I don't think you can open it."

Sandy slowly moved the knob, first to A and then clear around to Z. Next he pointed the arrow to 1 and then to 3. Nothing happened. He looked at the directions again. Yes, he had remembered them exactly:

> *If you know A from Z and 1 from 3*
> *Twist right or left to set me free.*

He tried it once more, this time working from left to right. But again nothing happened. The lock refused to give up its secret. Sandy twisted and turned the knob, slowly at first, then faster and faster until the arrow spun around the dial. The lock still held.

"That's not going to do any good," said Kit, a little amused by his brother's hard work but disappointed that Sandy had failed. "It's my turn now." He shouldered Sandy aside.

Because Kit was older than Sandy, he had more patience and worked more slowly. Under his deliberate fingers the arrow traveled back and forth and around and around the padlock. His face flushed and his fingers grew damp.

"Kit," said Sandy, peering over his shoulder, "I've got an idea. Why don't we try to spell out something on the dial?"

Kit leaned against the fireplace. "What will we spell?" He mopped his face.

"I dunno," Sandy answered. "It was just an idea."

"Let's begin with our names," said Kit with new interest. "Maybe Plum Nelly did set the dial that way."

Now the boys began working in earnest. Under their nimble fingers the arrow flew across the dial. They spelled out KIT and SANDY and JOHN, their father's name, and even PLUM NELLY. They tried their mother's name and the names of their school friends. Nothing happened. Sandy had the bright thought of spelling out AGROPELTER, but even that did not open the padlock.

"We're stuck," said Kit, after they had tried every name they could remember. "Doggone if Plum Nelly hasn't stumped us!"

"That's it! That's it!" yelled Sandy excitedly. "That's it! I *know* that's it!" He grabbed the lock.

"What's it?" Kit said. "What are you talking about, Sandy?"

"You said 'doggone' a minute ago," said Sandy. "We've forgotten Yellow Dog Dingo!"

The arrow moved again. D-I-N-G-O it spelled, and with the last letter came a sharp click. Kit, his patience gone, snatched at the lock to be the first to open the secret panel. To his great surprise, the padlock still held firm. "Now, what do you think of that?" Kit said. He sat down in Plum Nelly's armchair and, kicking off his shoes, tucked his feet tailor-fashion under him. Sandy squatted on the floor, his back against the rough stone of the fireplace. Both boys gazed at the stubborn padlock and at the panel it guarded.

"I wonder what's behind that?" Sandy looked at the tiny door, his face all puckered in thought.

Kit sighed. "It can't be anything very big. The panel isn't large enough for anything that's really big." He untwined himself and sauntered over to the fireplace. Once more the boys gazed at the mysterious panel that so far had baffled their best efforts.

Suddenly Sandy asked, "How old is Yellow Dog Dingo now?"

"He's three now," said Kit. "He was just a year when we got him. We've had two birthday parties for him. His last hamburger cake had three candles on—" Kit stopped abruptly, then turned to Sandy, his face all aglow with understanding. "That's the one and three, Sandy, I'm sure of it." He began twisting the padlock's dial knob—once to the left to stop at the figure 1 and then to the right to stop at 3. The padlock clicked—and opened!

"What's in there?" cried Sandy, pushing Kit aside. "Lemme get the door. Oh Kit! Look!" Sandy's usually cheerful voice turned into a wail as he pointed to the panel that now hung wide. No packages filled the dark cavity. This treasure cave seemed completely empty. "After all our work, and it's empty." Sandy's voice choked. He seldom cried, but now Kit saw that it took every effort for Sandy to hold back the tears.

Kit ran a hand back into the darkness that the panel had hidden, a hand that explored the interior stones and finally touched the back wall. There was something here after all! A birchbark envelope had been taped to the masonry. Kit worked it loose, then pulled it out. On the front was written: *For Kit and Sandy. Follow directions.*

"Hurry up and open it." Sandy forgot his tears. "Plum Nelly wasn't kidding us after all, was he?"

Several slips of paper tumbled out when Kit slit the flap; Sandy, his fingers all thumbs, scooped them up and spread them on the table. The boys weighted the slips down with a catsup bottle. Kit put a pepper mill, shaped like a miniature barrel, on the envelope, so that a breeze coming through the window would not blow the birchbark into the fireplace.

"What do they say?" asked Sandy, climbing on a chair to see better.

"Each paper tells us to do one thing every day," said Kit, busily rearranging the slips. "Here's today's, there's the one for tomorrow, and the next day's, and so on." He threw an arm around his brother, almost pushing him off the chair. "Get your cap and sweater. We're starting after today's treasure right now!"

"Where?" Sandy's voice came muffled by the sweater he was pulling over his head.

"In the old barn!" Kit replied, looking at one of the slips. He hurried out the door, and Sandy ran to keep up. "The directions say to hunt in the loft."

"What's a loft?"

"An attic," said Kit. "Can't you run faster?"

Plum Nelly's barn, once sound and tight against northern winters, now was only a shell—a forlorn place with boards that banged in the slightest wind and windows from which the glass had long been gone. Bats made it their home, and pack rats hid their stolen prizes beneath rotting floor boards. The boys edged through a litter of junk thrown carelessly about—broken tools, worn-out tires, an ancient boiler, a rusting snowplow. In the barn's far corner a ladder led to the loft. Kit boosted Sandy ahead of him, up into the gloomy second story. Below, the air was clean and sweet, but here beneath the rafters the place smelled musty. It was a queer smell, a mixture of decayed hay, old leather, and the hides of fur-bearing animals, which Plum Nelly cured in the loft.

"Phew!" said Sandy, holding his nose. A mouse rustled in his hay nest and ran in front of the boys. Sandy edged closer to Kit. He wasn't afraid of mice, he explained—he just didn't like them to surprise him that way. Kit nodded solemnly and led the way past a pitchfork, its tines rusted, and around a stack of hide stretchers to the far corner. An old cupboard stood there, but the shelves were bare.

"Oh," said Sandy in a small voice, wishing he were back in Plum Nelly's cabin.

"There's no use being afraid, Sandy," said Kit, with more confidence than he felt. "Now that we're up here, we might as well search everywhere." He started toward the ladder, scuffling piles of hay with his foot. "Maybe the treasure is buried under this stuff."

Sandy plucked at Kit's sleeve. "What's that?" He pointed to a gleaming white spot on the rafter.

"A pigeon," grunted Kit, not bothering to glance up. "Plum Nelly said they roost in here." He went on kicking hay.

Sandy stepped cautiously toward the white spot. He didn't want mice running across his feet, even though they were harmless. Step by step he moved away from Kit, finally reaching the rafter. This was no pigeon. It was a package wrapped in white paper! He pulled it down, and a shower of dust filled his eyes and made him sneeze.

Kit looked up. "What you making all that racket for?" He saw Sandy, eyes watering and nose running, holding the package. "Hurrah for you, Sandy. It wasn't a pigeon after all, was it?" Kit led Sandy toward the ladder. "Be careful now," he cautioned. "Wipe your eyes so you can see what you're doing."

Sandy backed down the ladder, his feet feeling for the rickety rungs. Without warning, a pair of strong hands caught him around the middle and swung him to the floor. Sandy, clutching the treasure, looked into Plum Nelly's beaming face.

"Great guns and sour pickles!" boomed Plum Nelly, giving Kit a hand down. "So you finally found it." Chuckling, Plum Nelly led the boys into an old box stall. "I call this my barn office," he explained. A workbench was strewn with tools. Three-legged milking stools served as chairs. "Here," said Plum Nelly, handing Sandy a knife. "Cut the string."

Two small boxes fell into Sandy's hands. "One's for Kit," Plum Nelly said. He acted as if opening jewel boxes in a stall were an everyday event at Broadwater. Kit pressed the catch on his box. There lay a compass, the red dot on its quivering needle pointing due north.

"I've got one, too, and it's a beauty," said Sandy.

"Best there is," Plum Nelly said proudly. "Sent to the city fer 'em. If you guys are goin' to be woodsmen, you gotta know how to use a compass."

"So that's why you asked us this morning if we had brought compasses with us," said Kit.

"Yup." Plum Nelly pointed to the gifts. "They're the best made—no fancy doodads on the dial, jest the major directions and the north end of the needle marked with a red dot, so there's no question which end points north." Plum Nelly was vastly pleased with himself. "Put 'em in your pocket now," he continued, "and don't go in the woods or on the lake without 'em." Plum Nelly looked stern. "Promise?" he said. The boys gave their word.

"Knew you would," said Plum Nelly, "but wanted to make sure." He paused as if uncertain what to say next. "'Course," he continued, "a compass just has to have north on it. Couldn't have a compass without north. Did I ever tell you about the days before north was discovered?" He fumbled for his tobacco pouch. "It's a tale I heard from the Indians, when I first came up here. Want to hear it?"

"Sure," chorused the boys.

"A long time ago," Plum Nelly began, puffing his pipe and settling back in his box-stall workshop, "there was an Indian princess who was very beautiful. All the braves of the tribe wanted to marry her. They brought her gifts of the finest pelts—glossy beaver, warm marten, and the soft fur of the snowshoe rabbit. In summer they kept her wigwam filled with blueberries. At the time of the Harvest Moon, the young men kept her and her old mother supplied with cranberries, fresh from the swamps. Other girls would have been spoiled with so much attention, but Walker-in-the-Pines—that was the princess's name—was not.

"She worked like any other maiden in the village, carving gourds into drinking cups and beating doeskin with a wooden mallet to make it soft for sewing. She helped her mother with the cooking, and played games with the younger children. She nursed the sick. She was very happy, for her father had been a chief, she was a princess, and she was courted by every warrior of the tribe. Everyone loved Walker-in-the-Pines, because her heart was good and true. Everybody loved her except one man, a swaggering know-it-all who spoke with a split tongue and cursed with the evil eye. He hated her because her heart pointed steadily to goodness and because Walker-in-the-Pines refused to marry him.

"And Evil Eye swore by the devils he knew to harm her, because she was good and because her heart was pure.

"He waited until the first day of the wild-rice harvest, when the gathering canoes moved slowly through the grain beds of the lakes. The stalks with their swollen rice heads were pulled over the sides of the canoe and the kernels were knocked off with paddles shaped for just that purpose. The harvest was plentiful. Walker-in-the-Pines sang a song of thanksgiving as she saw the grain piles growing bigger in the canoes of her people. There would be no hunger during the coming winter. The harvest was bountiful.

"Evil Eye called to Walker-in-the-Pines that he had found more rich beds. He told her to follow his voice. The princess, suspecting nothing, followed this bad warrior. He led her farther and farther from her people, in and out of inlets and across bays. Then he killed her, hiding her body where it was never found.

"Her spirit was so good that it winged its way straight

to the Happy Hunting Grounds. And as it went, all the things in the woods bowed their heads in the direction she went. The little ripples of the lake moved after her. The wild rice bent in the direction she took. The green moss on the forest trees moved from one side of the trees to the other. And even the pine needles pointed the way that Walker-in-the-Pines had taken.

"The Indians believed from that time on that a new star appeared in the sky of the north country and that this star was the best star of all because it always pointed to goodness and truth. They took it as their guiding point when they traveled. If sometimes the nights were dark and the star couldn't be seen, they took a pine needle and dropped it into a birch cup of water. When it stopped moving, it always pointed to Walker-in-the-Pines' star, far up there in the Happy Hunting Grounds.

"White men call this star the North Star, but the Indians call it Walker-in-the-Pines' star. And the Indians say that moss grows on the north side of trees because it moved there to point out the way the princess went that day when Evil Eye murdered her."

"Gee, that's a good story," Sandy said admiringly when Plum Nelly stopped.

"Yes, and it's a true Indian story," Plum Nelly answered. "You'll notice," he went on, "that the needle of your new compasses, like the floating pine needle, points due north." He smiled. "Perhaps Walker-in-the-Pines gave the white man his way to find north, too."

As Plum Nelly and the boys left the barn, they heard Yellow Dog Dingo bark joyously, and around the corner came Mr. Duncan, gun in hand and a pair of beautiful

grouse slung over his shoulder. "Chicken for supper tonight!" he called.

"And wild rice, too," said Plum Nelly."

"The kind of rice that Walker-in-the-Pines and her
tribe gathered?" asked Kit, patting Dingo, who was acting
as proud as if he had shot the grouse.

"The very same kind," said Plum Nelly. "The Indians
still gather it, and every autumn I buy some from them.
Now let's go and clean the game."

5 How Plum Nelly Met Paul Bunyan and How Yellow Dog Dingo Met His Waterloo

Plum Nelly led the way to the fishhouse, a screened shed about six feet square. Inside was a cleaning shelf and a pail for waste. A row of fish scalers and glittering knives hung on the wall. Plum Nelly cut off the heads and feet of the grouse. The boys watched, fascinated by the skilled, sure way Plum Nelly skinned the birds.

"Look," said Plum Nelly, "their crops are jest stuffed full of clover. And this fellow has been nibbling a mushroom."

Mr. Duncan peered over Plum Nelly's shoulder. "I thought they ate a lot of insects—like caterpillars."

"Oh, the young ones do," said Plum Nelly, picking stray pinfeathers. "They eat caterpillars, like you say, and ants and beetles. But after they grow up they prefer buds and leaves. They sure go for aspen and clover." He cleaned his knife and turned to Sandy. "Let's get after that crappie of yours now."

"Is it worth while to bother with just one fish, Plum Nelly?" Sandy asked. "We've got enough grouse for supper."

Plum Nelly didn't answer until he'd laid the crappie on the cleaning board. Then he turned to Sandy. "Your name isn't Tamarack Joe, is it?"

"No, of course not." Sandy didn't quite understand what Plum Nelly meant and he felt uneasy, for all the good humor was gone from Plum Nelly's face.

"I just wondered." Plum Nelly deliberately scaled the fish.

"Why?" said Kit, who felt something was wrong but didn't know why Plum Nelly should be irritated.

Plum Nelly laid the fish on a newspaper with the grouse. He brushed the scales and insides into the waste pail, and carefully wiped the cleaning shelf. He washed his hands. Yellow Dog Dingo came and scratched at the door. Plum Nelly paid no attention. The fishhouse was so silent that the boys could hear the lake slapping the shore rocks.

"Tamarack Joe," Plum Nelly said abruptly, "was a lazy, good-for-nothing, mealy-mouthed, wind-blown, ring-boned, swinney-eyed, pot-bellied Indian." He stopped for breath. The boys were wide-eyed; this was a different Plum Nelly.

"Yes, sir," said Plum Nelly, speaking to no one in particular but fixing stern eyes on Sandy, "this Tamarack Joe had a camp over on Girl Lake, beyond the point there. His place was dirty, and he was dirty. His squaw was dirty, and the kids were filthy.

"And he was as lazy a man as I ever laid eyes on. He was so confounded lazy he wouldn't build a fire to keep him from freezing to death. He wouldn't even keep his canoe patched. He'd squat in water rather than calk leaks. But Tamarack Joe did like to fish and hunt. If he worked at anything, he worked at that. But once he'd shot a duck or caught a fish, he'd be just as apt as not to ferget 'bout cleaning it. He'd say he didn't have time, or it warn't worth while to clean jest one critter. So his kind always was hungry. I've seen 'em many a time, beggin' for scraps to fill their pinched bellies. But that warn't all, no sir!" Plum Nelly started for the garbage dump with the waste pail.

Plum Nelly spoke over his shoulder. "Tamarack Joe destroyed wild life needlessly. No good woodsman does that." He stomped into the woods to the garbage pit, grumbling and grunting.

"Oh bro-*ther!*" said Kit. "He's sore as a boil."

"I'll say he is." Sandy tucked the crappie and grouse under an arm. "Has that guy got a temper! He's worse than my teacher. Jeepers!"

"Plum Nelly's not so bad," said Mr. Duncan. "All of us believe in conservation. We want to save game and not waste it. That way future Americans can enjoy the outdoors. Plum Nelly wasn't really angry with you. He's mad at people who come up here and waste game."

"That's right," Plum Nelly said, joining the boys. "It

was different, perhaps, years ago when game was plentiful
and when Paul Bunyan and I—"

"You didn't know Paul Bunyan, did you?" Sandy broke
in, almost dropping the game.

"Didn't know Paul? Now, what in tarnation makes you
think that? Of course I knew him. Logged with him a year,
I did." Plum Nelly stalked into the kitchen, the boys close
at his heels. The room was cooling, now that the sun was
going down. Plum Nelly busied himself at the stove. The
kindling caught with a roar, puffing up the pipe and settling down to a steady purr. A loon cried, his wailing laugh
a farewell to day and welcome to the night.

"I don't exactly remember the year," began Plum Nelly,
"but it was right after I quit the lake boats. Sailoring was
good enough for a spell, but I wearied of life on *The Flying
Cloud*. So I took my pay and come up here."

"And that's when you met Paul Bunyan?" Kit wanted to
hear more about the famous lumberjack of the north
woods, a man so mighty he had dug the St. Lawrence
River all by himself and stacked up the Black Hills. Paul
Bunyan was a powerful name in these parts. "Boy, will we
have something to tell when we get home," Kit whispered.
Sandy nodded, edging closer to Plum Nelly, who had sat
down and was warming his stocking feet on the oven door.

"You hear a heap of tales 'bout Paul and how he came
up here with his right-hand man, Johnny Inkslinger, and
Babe, the Blue Ox," said Plum Nelly, wiggling his toes.
"But, ter tell the truth, I don't take much stock in any of
it. Some things they tell about him are true enough—like
him loggin' the Big Onion and usin' a lake to make soup
in. And he had a laugh that when he'd let it out

would blow down a section of timber. That's true as gospel. But ole Paul never got down to the cow country like some liars say, and he never ventured out ter Puget Sound and dug it. It sure riles me, the way folks who never knew Paul talk about him."

Plum Nelly sighed and let his toes wiggle some more. He turned to Mr. Duncan. " 'Pears to me, John, you better be a-gettin' the victuals on. It's your turn to cook. Anyways, I'm goin' ter be powerful busy settin' these boys of yours straight on my old friend Paul."

"All right," Mr. Duncan chuckled, "but we're out of water. One of you boys will have to bring up a full bucket." He looked meaningfully at Kit, the kind of look a father uses when he means *Do this right away!*

"Gosh, Dad, I'll miss Plum Nelly's story if I go."

"I'll wait till you come back, Kit," said Plum Nelly. "Matter of fact, I've got a chore to do myself. Sandy can help me cut a piece of ice. Meant to do it earlier, but it plumb slipped my mind." He stuffed his warm toes into his boots. "Come on, Sandy, to the icehouse." Kit followed, bucket banging and his face twisted in such a frown that Plum Nelly said he looked like a he-coon with the colic. Kit sulked off toward the pump. Pretty soon Sandy heard the tin dipper clatter, and he knew Kit was priming the pump, which wouldn't draw unless a little water was poured into it first. *Screech, screech* went the pump.

"That old he-coon's getting water now," said Sandy as the racket stopped.

"Tck! tck!" said Plum Nelly, climbing a pile of sawdust-covered ice. He swept a cake clean with his hands and began to saw. "You shouldn't call your brother names."

"W-e-ll," Sandy spoke slowly, "maybe Kit isn't a he-coon, but . . . but he's a knucklehead! He'll get out of work every chance he gets. Say, Plum Nelly, where do you get all this ice?"

"Me and Uncle Bert and Boots chop it out of the lake every winter an' haul it up here over the snow on a sled. And then we shovel sawdust from the mill over it to keep it." Plum Nelly hefted fifty pounds with the ice tongs and came slipping and slithering down the pile. "This ought to be enough to cool the icebox for a day or so."

Kit was setting his bucket on the shelf below the tin wash basin when Sandy and Plum Nelly came back. A tea-kettle bubbled on the cherry-hot stove, breathing spurts of steam that covered the mirror with a thin mist. The cozy kitchen felt good, and the smell of grouse simmering whetted appetites.

Plum Nelly shook off his boots and fed an elm chunk to the stove. Propping his feet against the oven door, he looked around contentedly. The kitchen was a homey place, with onions drying from the rafters and a rocking chair near the stove. Plum Nelly closed his eyes.

"Hi!"

Plum Nelly jerked up.

"Don't go to sleep on us!" Sandy said. "You promised to tell us more about Paul Bunyan."

"You sure did," echoed Kit.

Plum Nelly grinned. "There's no rest for the wicked, I can see that." He yawned. "This air makes me sleepy. Let me see now . . . where was I?"

"You were telling us about Paul," said Kit, who didn't really remember just where Plum Nelly's story had stopped, but who wanted to get him started again. "We don't have to prime you like the pump, do we?"

"Nope," said Plum Nelly. "I was tellin' you that a lot of folk talk bosh about Paul Bunyan. They make him out to be a hero or somethin'. He sure enough was a good lumberjack, I'll say that fer him. Why, I remember jest as plain as day when I first met him. I was walkin' up north of here, scoutin' around fer timber fer myself, when I run smack agin' him. First thing I knowed, there he was, all done up in high boots an' plaid shirt. His head was brushin' the tips of the pine trees, an' his red cap was so high in the sky it looked like another sun riding the horizon. Some folks talk 'bout Paul like he was a giant, but he was just a big man. No bigger than most Americans—no bigger than the men who dug the Erie Canal or saved the Union or—"

"Gosh," said Sandy, and Mr. Duncan stopped to listen. Even Yellow Dog Dingo lifted his ears, though, being a hound dog, he couldn't lift them high.

"He talked real polite-like, too," Plum Nelly went on, "in a rumbling voice that made me think of thunder, though the day was clear an' the wind whistled from the west. He hunkered down on his heels so as to see me better, an' asked who I was an' where I come from. When I told him I was a sailor turned woodsman, he nodded and said he'd been accused of diggin' the Great Lakes, but he didn't remember doin' it if he had. He was common as an old shoe, settin' there fondling his wonderful gun with the curved barrel, and a beard hangin' down to the waist. He saw me admirin' his whiskers. 'Looks don't make the man,' Paul said to me, uprootin' an evergreen and slippin'

it into his vest pocket, which looked like a forest, filled as it was with other trees he was transplantin'."

"You mean his vest pockets were full of trees?" Sharp amazement filled Sandy's voice.

"O' course they were. Paul always was movin' trees around, plantin' 'em where his loggers had cut. That way new forests always wuz a-growin'. Shucks, we do the same thing today, only young trees are carried in trucks, not pockets."

Mr. Duncan, a dish towel aproned around his middle, turned from the range. "Replanting trees is a regular part of conservation, fellows—but I didn't know Paul Bunyan started it."

"Is that all? Didn't Paul say anything else?" asked Sandy.

"Yeah," said Kit, "what's that you said about a gun with a curved barrel? Why, that's impossible!" He glared at Plum Nelly, daring him to deny it.

Kit edged closer to the stove, for day had grayed into night, and with darkness a lake wind arose, rustling branches and whirling dry leaves. The evening chill that comes quickly in the north country during autumn and warns of winter pushed drafts under Plum Nelly's door and crept across the kitchen on quiet thief feet. Yellow Dog Dingo shivered in his dreams.

"So—so you don't believe that Paul Bunyan hunted with a curved barrel to his gun!" Plum Nelly pushed himself from his chair to peer out the window. He shook his head. "Likely to git a little snow most any day now. Lake's sure riled up an' that cussed wind is out of the east. Why don't you boys give your dad a hand with coffee makin'? I can yarn better with a mug in my hand."

How the boys hurried with the coffee! One fetched a cloth bag, another filled it with coffee, and both tried to tie the top at the same time. Sandy measured the water, and Kit popped the bag in and set the pot to boil.

"Now," they cried; "now the coffee's on. Now what about that blunderbuss with the curved barrel?"

"Well, as I was sayin'," drawled Plum Nelly, his eyes on the big gray pot that was bubbling and sending out fragrant odors, "Paul Bunyan and me got to be real friendly. We talked about plantin' crops, and he says the right time to put in corn was when an oak leaf is as big as a squirrel's foot. I told him I was powerful fond of succotash, and he sez his camp cook always used venison meat in mince pies. One thing led to another, jest neighborly chatter. He believed in herbs to cure colds, and I do too. Finally, with things goin' along so nice and pleasant, I asked him what happened to his gun. Said it was too bad he'd dropped and bent it like that. I said there was a smith down ter Hackensack that could fix it fer him, but likely he'd charge too much fer the job."

Plum Nelly poured a cup of coffee. "Nope, don't want no cow or sugar in it. I take 'er dark as blackstrap molasses. Well, you wouldn't believe it, but Paul laughed like anything when I asked about his gun. He said it warn't broke at all—that's the way he'd made it!" Plum Nelly smacked his lips.

"When Paul said his rifle wasn't broke, I almost fell over backwards; I guess I would have if I hadn't been leaning agin a tree. Who ever heard, like Kit here says, of a curved barrel? But when Paul explained things, I understood. It seems he'd been havin' a lot of trouble shootin' around corners with a straight barrel an' knockin' off a flight of mallards as they swung round the horizon. One day he tracked a bear clean round a mountain an' never caught sight of him. A musket with a curved barrel would've solved his problem.

"So he got himself a cannon from the Revolutionary War and took the breech out of it. That was the start of the most famous rifle in America. Oh, I know a heap of folks think the Kentucky rifle was the finest made. But Paul's gun beat it all hollow. Not even Dan'l Boone could shoot round corners the way Paul did. He forged the barrel himself, bending it in a half circle when it was blisterin' hot. He raided Wisconsin's lead mines to make bullets as big as a giant's fist. He sent all the way to Pennsylvany fer casks of blackest powder, and he got sharpest flints from along Gunflint Trail, way up near the Canadian border.

"It took Paul nigh on a year to pattern Old Smokey. The first time he shot her off, he wasn't aimin' at anything—just tryin' her out. The next afternoon a runner come pantin' up, sayin' ten thousand ducks had fell out of the air three counties away! That was enough mallards fer two meals for Paul's loggers. Sourdough Sam, Paul's cook, worked seventeen days jest to dress them ducks and three weeks more pickin' pinfeathers. Paul said he guessed Old Smokey worked real good. After he got Old Smokey, he never used a regular gun again. That's what he told me the day I met him in the woods."

"Soup's on!" called Mr. Duncan. "Come and get it or I'll throw it out!"

Yellow Dog Dingo yawned, stretched himself, and trotted to the door, his tail waving. "Don't be gone long," said Kit, "and don't tangle with Mr. Porcupine."

"He's too smart for that." Sandy pushed a chair to the table and helped himself to fish and grouse. He smothered his potatoes with gravy.

"Oh, I don't know," Kit said. "Hey, pass me some, too. You think you're the only one eating?"

"He-coon!" Sandy was safe at the far end of the table.

"I'm not!"

"You are!"

Kit beat his fist on the table. "You're the coon!"

"Sez you!"

"Yah, sez me!"

Without saying a word, Plum Nelly vanished into the bunkroom. The boys heard him opening and shutting drawers. The closet door banged. He came back and flung two sets of boxing gloves on the table—old, scuffed gloves, but heavy enough to do wicked damage to a boy's nose. "If you fellers want to start a war, take these out behind the barn. But don't expect me to save supper fer you. Make yer choice now—fight or eat!" Plum Nelly helped himself to grouse.

"Aw," said Sandy, "I was only fooling!"

"Me too!" Kit reached for the bread plate. "I really wasn't mad at Sandy, I only—"

Just then, far back in the timber, Yellow Dog Dingo howled, a wailing howl that rose and fell like a siren.

"What the—" Mr. Duncan shoved back his chair. The howl was nearer and louder. It changed to a scream and a wail and back to a pitiful howl. "Do you suppose that fool dog has run into a panther?"

Plum Nelly slipped a shell into his deer rifle and they all stepped outside. "Could be." He listened as the howls came closer. "But my guess is Dingo's got a snootful of porcupine quills. He's sure headin' fer home."

"Maybe he got caught in a trap," suggested Mr. Duncan.

"Don't think so," grunted Plum Nelly. "He wouldn't be travelin' this fast with iron hanging on his leg."

"Phew!" Sandy said suddenly.

"Bro-*ther*, oh bro-*ther*," moaned Kit, jumping up and down and holding his nose.

The hound broke through the woods behind the garbage pit, circled the fishhouse, and, with tail drooping, headed straight for the cabin. With every step he yelled louder. The wind carried Dingo's smell ahead of him, a stink that caught Sandy by the throat, choking him.

"Lord in heaven!" cried Mr. Duncan. "That fool hound has tangled with a skunk. PHEW!" He turned swiftly to the boys. "Get in the house, you two, before he rubs that stuff on you, or I'll never be able to take you home!"

As Plum Nelly and Mr. Duncan watched, Dingo skittered to a stop, bent his tail under him, and lifted a skunk-drenched face to the heavens. A great mournful bugling told of his tragedy: how he'd gone forth joyfully and full of ginger to nose new wood smells; how that long nose of his caught the scent of cottontail and snowshoe rabbit and scampering gopher; how suddenly he came upon a strange striped animal with bushy tail held proudly over back; how he danced up to it, wanting nothing more than to be friendly; and—how this miserable thing had tricked him, soaking him with a spray that burned his eyes and smelled a thousand times worse than the city dump back home. All this, and more, poor Yellow Dog Dingo poured forth. The forest rang with his grief. Then he rolled over and over, rubbing his back on a mat of pine needles and leaves. He got up, started to bark, changed his mind, and scrubbed his face on the ground, scattering leaves like a hurricane.

"C'mon, Dingo," said Plum Nelly.

The dog crept closer cautiously, knowing that he was no proper company for anyone. Disgrace showed big in his eyes.

Mr. Duncan turned away, a handkerchief to his face. "Jumping Jehoshaphat! How he stinks! Phew!" Dingo mourned at him. *Don't say that,* he begged.

"C'mon, boy," Plum Nelly repeated, catching Dingo by the collar and hustling him off to the barn. "Every city dog has to learn some time or other." Mr. Duncan followed, and behind him trailed Kit and Sandy, who just couldn't stay in the cabin when all this excitement was going on. But they were mighty careful to keep a long, long way from Yellow Dog Dingo.

"What are you going to do to him?" asked Sandy.

"Will he ever get over it?" interrupted Kit, who loved Dingo with all his heart.

"Sure," grunted Plum Nelly, "but not till he's had a bath. Run into the house, Kit, and get me a dozen cans of tomatoes."

"Tomatoes?"

"That's what I said. Canned tomatoes!"

"Will tomatoes do any good?" Sandy plucked his father's sleeve.

"As sure as eggs is eggs," said Mr. Duncan.

"But Dingo doesn't like tomatoes," wailed Sandy.

"We're going to bathe him with 'em," put in Plum Nelly, "not feed 'em to him."

"Now I've heard everything!" Disbelief showed plain on Sandy's face.

Kit, his arms piled with cans, hurried back. An opener stuck out from the pocket of his windbreaker. "I'll open them for you," he panted.

As fast as Kit handed a can to Plum Nelly, the tomatoes were rubbed into Dingo's hair and worked down to the pink skin. From tip of tail to tip of nose, Dingo was washed. At first the dog fought like a wild bronco, bucking, jumping stiff-legged, and sunfishing. Neck hair stood on end like a lion's, and deep belly growls rumbled up. Gradually he quieted under Plum Nelly's skilled hands, understanding, as dogs do, that he was being helped.

Finally Plum Nelly straightened up. "That does it. Now I'll rinse him with cold water and let him sleep in the barn tonight."

"Gee, Plum Nelly," said Sandy, after forlorn Dingo had been put to bed, "you smell, too."

"Something rotten in Denmark, eh?" Plum Nelly tousled Sandy's hair. "You just watch me!"

As he spoke, Plum Nelly slid out of his jacket and slipped out of faded jeans. Off came the woolen shirt with its brilliant plaids. The long underwear was shucked the way a snake sheds its skin in the spring. And there stood Plum Nelly, jay-bird naked except for socks and shoes. These, too, were discarded. The chilly night nipped at Plum Nelly, raising goose pimples there in the moonlight. Kit shivered just to see them.

Plum Nelly flapped his arms, prancing like a scarecrow, then danced like a clumsy bear holding a tin cup. "I'm the original streak of lightnin'," he howled, cutting a turkey-wing. "I'm half hoss an' half alligator, an' I kin lick my weight in wildcats. I kin grin the bark off a tree an' I—" He broke off, grinning sheepishly. "—an' I'm cold," he finished. He pell-melled into the cabin to hug the range.

Behind Plum Nelly's back, Sandy beckoned Kit into the bunkroom. "Man, oh man! Did you see those muscles?"

"He's built like a bison," said Kit, whose sharp eyes had raced over Plum Nelly's body, taking in the compact chest, muscular frame, and sinewy arms. "Like a regular old bull bison. He's no runt like we first thought."

"Heck, no! He'd make the team any day. He's as tough as jerked buffalo!"

Plum Nelly, snorting and splashing like a seal, was squeezed in a washtub tighter than a sardine. Mr. Duncan sloshed hot water over his head and down his back. Every time the water hit him Plum Nelly roared. Now and then a lather-covered arm darted over the tub's side and grabbed a bottle of vinegar.

"Great guns and sour pickles," roared Plum Nelly, wiggling and writhing, "there's nothin' like water an' vinegar to soak skunk off a man. Blast that polecat anyways. Wow! That water's too danged hot! Take it easy, John!"

The boys couldn't keep from laughing, seeing the

mighty Plum Nelly all coiled like a hedgehog in the too-small tub, water scalding him, soap blinding him, and lather crisscrossing his brown body in white rivulets.

"Quit your wiggling," warned Mr. Duncan, lifting a fresh kettle. "The floor looks like Noah's flood hit it."

"I'm done!" Plum Nelly shot from the tub as if a wasp had sunk its stinger into him. He grabbed a towel. "You boys git to bed. Scram! Vamoose! Tomorrow's another day. And don't fret about Dingo; tomatoes are the thing fer what ails him!"

Long after the boys had turned in, Sandy heard a noise behind the cabin. He peeked out. There was Plum Nelly shuffling along, his smelly clothes held in front of him on a pitchfork. A long-handled shovel swung from one hand. "Bro-*ther*," said Sandy aloud, "I'm sure glad we didn't have to bury Yellow Dog Dingo."

6 *Fringed Buckskin and*
Pickled Pigs' Feet

"Sandy! Stir your stumps. C'mon now, get up! It's almost seven." Lazy Sandy wriggled deeper into his blankets.

Kit poked him. "C'mon, rise and shine! Do you think we've got all day? The treasure slip says we're to hunt where 'fairies scatter fern seed.'"

Sandy's eyes came briefly up from the covers. "There aren't any fairies," he said, and ducked down. "Lemme alone; I'm tired."

"Great guns and pickled pigs' feet! Who in this house

says there's no little people?" Plum Nelly ripped the blankets off Sandy and swept him to the floor. "Now then," Plum Nelly ordered, "git your jeans on, and I mean *git!*" Plum Nelly steered the sleepy-eyed youngster to his clothes. "No fairies, indeed! How would this north country ever have been settled without Lady Luck? Who but a fairy could lay the gold on a sunfish, paint the bass's back, or color the northern lights? Jest answer me that! Nobody can live up here without knowin' there's magic in the woods."

Poor Sandy hemmed and hawed and finally said he guessed maybe it was so, but that, so help him, he'd never seen an elf or a gnome, much less a real fairy with gossamer wings.

"Them that has eyes and see not," muttered Plum Nelly, banging out of the bunkroom.

"Now what do you suppose he meant by that?" Sandy fumbled into a shirt.

"I dunno," answered Kit. "But why couldn't you have kept your big mouth shut? Plum Nelly usually knows what he's talking about, and there's no use riling him up."

All through breakfast Sandy was unusually silent, although the buckwheat cakes were golden light and the bacon golden brown. He didn't even grab for seconds before anyone else, as he generally did. And he didn't forget to fold his napkin when the meal was over. This was so unusual that Mr. Duncan started to say something, but when he noticed the frown on Sandy's face he kept still.

"Let's go, bird-brain," said Kit, after he had tucked his ninth pancake away. For once Sandy didn't resent his brother's teasing, but meekly followed him to the barn to visit Yellow Dog Dingo. Dingo yapped gleefully when the boys untied him. "Umph," said Kit, "he doesn't smell too strong. Those tomatoes did the trick all right."

Sandy nodded listlessly, his mind on something else. "Say"—he brightened suddenly—"what's fern seed got to do with fairies, huh?"

"Plum Nelly says fern seed makes things invisible."

"How can we find treasure that's invisible? Just answer me that!"

"You're sharper than a cap pistol this morning," said Kit, watching Yellow Dog Dingo chase a saucy chipmunk. "Here comes Plum Nelly. Let's have some fun with him. Say, Plum Nelly, where can Sandy and I get some fern seed?"

"Where there's fern, I reckon." Plum Nelly swept a hand toward the barn. "Behind there used to be a pretty good bank of 'em, but they're frosted brown this time of year. I got ter dip the dead minnows out of my tank. You can find the spot easy enough." He walked on to the boathouse with never a look behind.

"He's a big help," Sandy said.

Kit puckered his forehead. "Maybe so, maybe not. Let's go look for that frost fern anyway."

Kit's new compass showed their route as north by west. Behind the barn lay barren ground, and beyond that the boys pushed through underbrush and scrub oak. The path grew more difficult, tall trees and squat evergreens hampering their movements. Here the ground lay in deep shade, carpeted with leaves that rustled and whispered beneath their feet. Sandy was climbing over a tangled windfall when the earth in front of him exploded. *Zoom!* A bird that Sandy thought three times as big as the biggest eagle and eleven times larger than a B-29 flushed away, dodging in and out of trees and disappearing over a hill. Sandy's heart beat so hard he held it in place with his hand. Kit stuttered weakly, "Wha . . . what was that?"

Sandy swallowed his heart for the seventh or eighth time. "A little grouse, but it sure scared the daylights out of me."

The boys plunged deeper into the forest. Like all tenderfeet, they crashed through underbrush, stumbled over deadfalls, and made so much noise that every living woodthing was warned. The boys were so busy dodging branches and stepping over fallen logs that they failed to see the animals who watched their clumsy progress. A deer peered through a lattice of vines, then minced shyly into a thicket. Brother bear, snuffling berries, watched with humorous eyes. A porcupine, as brave in quills as a knight in armor, did not even bother to run. And a partridge blended herself with the grass not five feet away from them. Kit and Sandy saw none of these creatures. To them the forest seemed empty.

"Jim-iny crickets," complained Sandy, flopping down. "I'm bushed. How much farther do you suppose those ferns are? Maybe they're invisible, too." His face grew long and gloomy. "Say, we're not lost, are we, Kit?"

Kit shook his head. "I don't think so; leastways we're not all the way lost. I mean, we can get back to Plum Nelly's all right, but I don't know if I can find the ferns."

"Seems to me we've gone miles and miles." Sandy climbed to his feet.

"Not that far, but a good two miles, I'd guess. It can't be much farther now."

"Well," Sandy grumbled, "it's a lot farther than Plum Nelly let on to us."

Kit climbed a hummock slippery with frost. "There's a creek over there and a high bank. I bet that's where Plum Nelly meant." He looked more carefully. "Sandy! The road's on the other side of the bank. We could have walked it and found the ferns just as easy as pie!"

"Jeepers! We sure came the hard way."

In a few minutes the boys jumped the trickle that was a creek, climbed a fern-covered bank, and stood on Plum Nelly's land.

"Well," puffed Kit, "Plum Nelly sure pulled the wool over our eyes. But there's fern here, all right. The only difficulty," he went on, "is that I don't see any fern seed. This stuff looks all brown and withered to me. What's that?"

A jeep, side curtains flapping, jitterbugged down the road. It snorted to a stop. "Hi, fellers! Find any fern seed yet?"

"Plum Nelly! Why didn't you tell us we could come by the road instead of traipsing through the woods?" Kit asked.

"Yeh," Sandy echoed. "And why didn't you say you were coming? We could have ridden along."

"Well, it's this way. It's always a good thing in the woods to ask the best way to git somewhere. I said the fern seed wuz behind the barn, an' you guys lit out without sayin' a word. I reckon you've learned your lesson now." Plum Nelly slid out of the jeep. "Find yer seed yet?"

"This stuff is all brown and withered," Kit said disgustedly. "Seed's been blown off for a long time."

"Faint heart never won fair lady," answered Plum Nelly, not at all bothered by Kit's disgust. "That's what they used to say when I was a boy."

"Oh, well, I suppose we can look, now that we're here." Kit motioned to Sandy. "You go along the bank that way, and I'll go this."

"That's the old fight," said Plum Nelly, apparently much pleased. "Never kin tell what a crow will pick up in a corn field." He climbed back into the jeep. "I'll wait fer you."

Sandy disappeared, and Kit picked his way slowly along the bank. He didn't know just what he was searching for, but he wouldn't give Plum Nelly the satisfaction of asking.

Kit poked along, crumpling leaves in his hands and yanking up roots. Did ferns have seeds underground, like potato eyes? Were they on stalks like berries? He didn't know. Then, right there in front of him lay a long cardboard box, all neatly covered with fern so as to be almost invisible. Brushing the fern away, Kit saw lettering done in crayon: "For Kit and Sandy."

"I've got it! Jumpin' creepers! I've found the treasure." Kit sprinted to the jeep with the box. "Look, Sandy," he said as his brother ran up, "it's a big box and it was covered with fern. I almost missed it."

"Well, don't jest stand there. Open it!"

"Okay, Plum Nelly, I'm going to." Kit's fingers plucked at the tough cord.

"Will you look at that!" Sandy unfolded a buckskin hunting shirt with deep patch pockets and fringed bottom. Kit pulled out another. The shirts were soft as a fawn's back, and fit the boys perfectly.

"Thanks, Plum Nelly, thanks a million. Where did you get 'em? They're beautiful." The boys climbed into the jeep, hurling questions at Plum Nelly.

"You sure look like a couple of Dan'l Boones," said Plum Nelly, grinding the starter. "Ain't nothin' like buckskin for the woods. No, sir!" The jeep whipped into a sharp turn. "I shot those deer myself, tanned the hides myself, and had 'em made up. Want to know how I shot 'em?"

"Sure," said Sandy, so busy admiring himself he almost tumbled out.

Plum Nelly eased the jeep's bucking. "It was this way. One cold morning about two years ago I had a taste in my mouth for venison. There comes a time when nothin' but venison will satisfy winter hunger. I'm one for creature comfort an' I didn't relish trampin' the woods that day. It was twenty below by the glass, and a foot or more of snow lay on the ground. One minute I'd decide to go, and the next I'd make up my mind I wouldn't. I fiddled and fooled around that way, most all day. Finally I strapped on my snowshoes and lit out, thinkin' what an idiot I was to leave my warm kitchen.

"I picked up the tracks of a big buck right over behind that ridge we're comin' to. Follered him a couple of miles and lost him in the swamp. By then it was purty dark, and I was ready to quit, when off behind a clump of firs I thought I seen somethin' movin'. And by jingo, here comes a buck ploddin' along through the snow. Right behind him was another. The second deer had the first buck's tail in his mouth and was being led.

"I've seen lots of things in the woods, but nothin' like

that, I can tell you. Then it came to me. That second deer was snow blind. The first deer was guiding him home. Quick as a wink, I shot the first buck dead. Then I run up, stuck my red necktie in the blind deer's mouth, and led him right back to the cabin easy as pie. I had my meat on the hoof. Nothin' to it, if you know how." The jeep leaped forward in a burst of speed.

"What happened to the first deer, the one you shot in the woods?" Kit shouted.

"Oh," said Plum Nelly, sweeping past the mail truck with horn squeaking, "next morning I went out an' toted him in. You got his skin on now, Sandy."

"That's one story I don't believe." Sandy was firm. "Deer don't get snow blind. And you wouldn't shoot a blind, defenseless animal. I know that, Plum Nelly. How did you really get these skins?"

"A pretty thing when you don't believe a mighty hunter!" Plum Nelly wasn't at all ashamed by the whopper he had just spun out of whole cloth. He was quiet a minute. "Guess I'll have to tell the truth. It was this way. One cold morning 'bout two years ago—"

"Plum Nelly!" Kit warned.

"—'bout two years ago," continued Plum Nelly, ignoring Kit's warning, "I was settin' in my rocker by the stove, thinkin' I'd better lay in meat. It was evening and—"

"Plum Nelly, are you sure this is going to be the real story of how you got these skins?" Sandy asked.

"As sure as pigs make bacon!"

"All right, then," Sandy said.

"As I was saying before I was rudely interrupted," Plum Nelly began, "I was just turning out the evening lamp when I happened to look out the window. There was a deer, lookin' in." The jeep shuddered, jouncing over bumps. "I fired right between his eyes. Strangest thing I ever see. He just melted away. Then he was back, and I let him have it again. Well, you won't believe it, but I'll have you know I shot that blasted animal nine times. And then I quit. If I couldn't bring down an ordinary two-for-a-nickel deer in nine shots, I'd better stop hunting.

"Next mornin' I went out behind the slab pile. Would you believe it, I found nine dead deer! But that wasn't all." Plum Nelly shoved his cap to the back of his head, scratching the bald spot. "Maybe you won't believe this, but it's true as gospel. Like I say, deer are smarter than a lot of people. The next night those deer fooled me plenty. They didn't like the way I was killin' 'em so fast." He chuckled, stepping hard on the gas. The boys clung tighter. "Well, like I said, the next night they come up again, only this time they was in pairs. Each deer would close one eye, and like the night before, I aimed right 'twixt the eyes. That's the way to kill deer. But when I shot between the eyes, I shot between the two deer that were holdin' their heads together. Missed every blame one of 'em. That taught me how smart deer are. But I had the nine deer anyways, and made your shirts from their hides!"

Plum Nelly looked at the boys out of the corners of his eyes. No one said anything for long minutes. The jeep swept around a thank-you-ma'am curve and headed for Broadwater, a hundred squeaks protesting the way Plum Nelly drove.

Finally, Kit, thinking hard and choosing his words carefully, faced Plum Nelly. "I guess Sandy and I just better give up." He shook his head. "There's no use trying to get a straight story out of you. You know you're just kidding us!"

Plum Nelly pulled up in front of the barn and got out. "Umph," he said, "I got witnesses to prove it. Uncle Bert seen me dressing out those deer. And if I hadn't got 'em, how could you fellows be wearin' new shirts now? Just answer me that!" He disappeared toward the dock, muttering, "Great guns and pickled pigs' feet" in a most disgusted voice.

"What do you suppose Plum Nelly says that all the time for?" Sandy asked as he started for the cabin.

"I dunno." Kit's mind was so filled with his new shirt that he paid little attention to Sandy.

"Don't know what?" Mr. Duncan stuck his head out of the door. Behind him, Yellow Dog Dingo whined a welcome.

"Don't know why Plum Nelly says 'great guns and picked pigs' feet' all the time," answered Sandy. "How do you like our new shirts? Pretty nifty, huh, Pop?"

Mr. Duncan smiled. "So you found them. I was afraid Plum Nelly's invisible fern seed would throw you off the track. Where's the old rascal now?"

"Hi, Dad!" Kit said. "They're sure swell shirts. Oh, Plum Nelly went down to the dock for something. He told us the worst tales about getting the skins for our shirts. Say, can I have a sandwich or something? I'm starving!"

"Me, too!" chimed in Sandy, who was always ready to eat. "Do you know why Plum Nelly keeps talking about pickled pigs' feet, huh?"

"Yes," said his father, "I know. It's a long story. I'll tell you after I fix a peanut-butter sandwich for each of you, but why you're hungry in the middle of the morning is more than I know. Aren't you ever filled up, Sandy?"

"No, sir," Sandy said solemnly, taking half his sandwich at one bite.

"Now, about this pigs' feet business . . ." Mr. Duncan looked to see if Plum Nelly was still on the dock. . . . "I guess it's all right to tell you, but never let on to Plum Nelly. It happened a long time ago, before I started coming up here. Plum Nelly didn't have this cabin; he was roughing it in a lean-to he'd put up on Pew's Point. Things weren't going any too well for him, I guess.

"Anyway, he had mighty little money and a mighty lot of places to spend what he had. One day, early in December, just before Broadwater froze over, he decided to hike into town for winter provisions. He ordered this and that—you know: coffee and flour and such stuff. And he included a keg of salt pork. You can do almost anything in the woods with salt pork. The order was to go out with a load for a lumber camp about thirty miles from here. The driver promised to set Plum Nelly's things off down here a mile or so from this cabin. Only the cabin, as I told you, wasn't built yet. Plum Nelly would pick up the order and tote it out to the Point. He had to get it down before heavy snowfall. Once a big snow came, he was shut in for the winter—no getting to town, no going anywhere. That was all right with Plum Nelly. He didn't care if he didn't go to town or see a white man all winter, as long as his lean-to was snug and he had enough grub.

"The wagon driver set the stuff off all right, and Plum

Nelly lugged it out to the Point in a snowstorm. The storm turned into a blizzard. Next morning there were four or five feet on the ground. Plum Nelly knew he was marooned, but he told me he didn't care much.

"Then he began checking over his grocery order, piling the stuff in one corner of the lean-to and covering it with old buffalo robes. The wind sure whistles around the Point, and Plum Nelly was happy as a beaver in a house. He had lots of firewood split, a strong lean-to, and plenty to eat. He could get along.

"When he pried off the top of the keg of salt pork, I guess he must have had fits, from what he told me. The storekeeper had sent him a keg—pounds and pounds—of pickled pigs' feet instead of salt pork! A woodsman can do almost anything with salt pork; without it he can't cook a thing. Salt pork is food and flavoring, main dish and dessert all rolled into one. But what can an outdoor cook do with pigs' feet? Tell me that!" Mr. Duncan turned to Sandy.

"I don't know. What did Plum Nelly do?"

"He ate pigs' feet," Mr. Duncan said emphatically. "I guess he had pickled pigs' feet for breakfast, pigs' feet for dinner, and pigs' feet for supper! Plum Nelly said he had pigs' feet in his bread, pigs' feet in soup, pigs' feet in the coffee. He got to hate pigs' feet—"

"Sure don't blame him," said Kit. "He can't forget them, either, can he?"

"Forget pigs' feet! I should say not," said Mr. Duncan. "He took an oath, out there on the Point with snow seven feet high, that he'd never eat another in this world or the next. He ate them from December through April, and that's more than enough in any man's life. He still gets riled up thinking about them, and whenever he's upset or excited or anything, why, he says, without knowing he's saying it, 'Great guns and pickled pigs' feet!' "

"So that's why," said Sandy, spreading another sandwich.

"That's why what?" Kit asked.

"Great guns and pickled pigs' feet," Sandy said disgustedly, "don't you ever listen—"

"Stop it, you two!" Mr. Duncan shouted. "I won't have another person around here saying that!"

"Saying what, Dad?" Kit asked innocently.

"Saying 'Great guns and pickled—' Oh no, you don't! Beat it, both of you."

"A fellow can't say *anything* around here," moaned Sandy, sliding out the door. "GREAT GUNS AND PICKLED PIGS' FEET!"

7 Collaring a Wolf Pack

The snow came out of the north: first a scattered advance guard feeling its way over the bay and into the forest. Behind these silent scouts moved the main army, regiment after regiment. By midday the invasion was complete, but snow still fell—endless white paratroopers dropping in formation from the sky.

Sandy, peering through frosted panes, was bored, for the storm had begun in early morning. Impatient and not knowing what to do with himself, he turned to Plum

Nelly, sprawled in the rocker with feet on a bear hide foot-stool. "What can a fellow do, cooped up in weather like this?" Sandy scratched at the frost to see better. "Me and Kit planned a hike."

"Reckon there's nothin' anybody can do about the weather." Plum Nelly yawned, watching Sandy's disappointment. "Me, I kinda like snow; can't do no outside chores and can laze around inside. Suits me fine." Plum Nelly closed his eyes, only to pop them open again. "Where's Kit and your dad?"

"Napping."

"Now, that's a fine thing." Plum Nelly raised his voice. "You two goin' to sleep all day? There's such a thing as being too lazy in a storm. Besides, I want to ask Sandy somethin'. Come on in."

Drowsily Mr. Duncan and Kit ambled from the bunk-room. Kit spread himself on the floor beside Yellow Dog Dingo, burying his face in the dog's warm fur.

"I'm bored, too," said Kit. "Gosh, it must be awful to live up here all winter." He looked quickly at Plum Nelly, adding, "I didn't mean to hurt your feelings, but being snowbound is hard to get used to."

"Snowbound!" laughed Plum Nelly. "You don't think we're snowbound, do you? Why, there's only an inch or so on the ground now. That's nothing, and it won't stay long. I'm used to eight feet—and more, some winters. Trouble with you city folk," he continued, getting up steam, "is that you don't know how to live by yourselves. Great guns and sour pickles! When I first came up here, I lived by myself and didn't see a white man from October till June. I fought wolves barehanded, and clubbed bears to make me an overcoat. There weren't no roads—no nothin'. Why, I remember a Swede and his family trying to get through this country with a horse and wagon. The whole outfit tumbled into a mudhole and wuz lost—all but the youngest child. When he managed to work himself out, he was forty-seven years old!"

"That must have been some winter." Sandy flopped down by Kit and Dingo.

"Oh, it wasn't too bad," said Plum Nelly modestly. "Of course, I did have a little trouble, but in some ways the cold made livin' easier. I remember, for instance, how I made my winter's supply of pancakes and stacked 'em up outside to freeze. When I wanted cakes of a mornin' I'd ax off a length and toss 'em on the griddle. Saved myself a lot of time.

"Some nights it got chilly enough to pull the nails right out of the barn, but I never let it bother me none. When the wind blew the other way, it pushed 'em right back in agin. Folks don't believe it, but it's true. Cold does strange things.

"It was jest such a day as this when I decided to shoot ducks. I stood up on the ridge yonder and watched them come over—teal, mallards, bluebills, anything you'd want. Them that flew over the ridge I let go. Them that was headin' this side of the ridge I shot, being careful to have 'em fall on the down slope toward the cabin. When those ducks began rollin' in the soft snow, they rolled themselves up in snowballs and come to a stop by the barn. I jest walked down the hill, piled the duck-balls up, and let 'em stay. Whenever I wanted a fresh duck, I'd crack one of the balls open, and there he'd be. Saved myself a lot of

work that way. I even trained icicles to grow over the back
roof. Never had to carry no water all winter. Just broke off
a bunch of stalks and set 'em on the stove. Frozen water
is better than the sweetest spring water, especially in winter
if a feller has to pail-carry. And Uncle Bert froze cordwood
shadows and burned 'em when wood got scarce. Said they
gave good heat and were a heap lighter to carry."

Plum Nelly burst into song, his voice sounding like a
file rubbing iron.

> *"A strange fish was the Whirligig;*
> *'Twas not so small and not so big.*
> *About ice holes these fish appeared*
> *Which had with bacon rind been smeared;*
> *They'd follow round these once or twice*
> *And whirl themselves out on the ice."*

"Hey, Plum Nelly! You don't have to sing to wake me
up. You sound like a screech owl!" Kit scrambled to his
feet. "Don't sing any more!"

"What's the matter with my singin'?" Plum Nelly asked.
"Did you ever hear the one about the—"

"No more, please, or I'll go out and lose myself in the
snow," Kit threatened.

"That's about all the sense you have," snorted Plum
Nelly. "All right, I won't sing. But did you ever hear the
one that goes like this?" Before either boy could stop him,
Plum Nelly threw back his head.

> *"Ten thousand Swedes*
> *Ran through the weeds*
> *Chased by one Norwegian.*

The dust of the weeds
Made snuff for the Swedes
At the battle of Copenhagen."

"Whoa!" shouted Sandy. "No, I never heard a song like that before. My music teacher would give me fits if she even knew I'd listened to it."

Plum Nelly grunted. "Don't know nothin' about that, but that's the singin' the boys did when I was lumberjackin'." He smiled, memory bringing back the old days when he was young enough and strong enough to swing an ax all day in the big woods and have energy enough left to dance all night. "There's nothin' wrong with good, honest music."

"Didn't you want to ask me something, Plum Nelly?" Sandy asked, anxious to stop more saw-tooth music.

"Guess I did, at that. Oh, yes, now I recollect." Plum Nelly nodded vigorously. "But I ought to ask your dad and Kit—they're the ones who nap all the time." Plum Nelly turned to Kit, who wondered what was going to happen. "Why," said Plum Nelly slowly, "are lazy persons' beds too short for them?"

Kit thought and thought, then shook his head.

"Give up?" Plum Nelly asked gleefully.

"Yup."

"Me too," said Sandy.

"And me," added Mr. Duncan, who was never good at riddles.

Plum Nelly pointed at Kit and his father. "Because they are too long in them!"

"Oh, bro-*ther*," whispered Kit to Sandy, "that's worse

than his singing. Let's get him started on something else."

"Okay." Sandy couldn't think of a thing to ask Plum Nelly. Suddenly he got an idea. "Say, Plum Nelly, are there wolves up here? Me an' Sandy were wondering," he added.

"Wolves!" exploded Plum Nelly. "Wolves! You should've seen the critters when I first took this place. Wolves and bears and owls that hooted all night and even a panther or so. Yes, sir, even panthers. Why, I remember like it was yesterday a trip I made into town with a sleigh and team. First thing I did when I prospered a mite was to git a pair of horses. Made the sleigh myself—even hammered out the runners at the Longville blacksmith's. Mighty good job, if I say so myself.

"As I was sayin', I started home from town this November morning with my groceries. I hustled to git the team hitched and was down the road three quarters of a mile or so before I remembered I'd left my rifle in Eric's store. But shucks, who'd need a gun jest comin' home on a peaceful morning? Hatrack and Mr. Bones were in fine fettle, lifting their feet graceful as a dancer and skimming the sleigh over the snow at a pretty pace. I reckon we'd gone two, mebbe three miles when Mr. Bones laid back his ears and snorted, the way a horse does when something's not to his fancy. 'What in tarnation is the matter with you, Mr. Bones, you old goat,' I sez, sticking my head out of my bearskin coat.

"The old horse didn't say nothin', which was strange, because he usually spoke right up when asked. He and Hatrack jest lit out fer home, the barn, and a measure of oats. Leastways, that's what I thought then. The road sure was pretty, all lined with firs and evergreens, with bright snow decoratin' them so as they looked like Christmas trees shining in the sun."

Plum Nelly shifted his rocker closer to the stove. "Then I see what was troubling the team. Timber wolves wuz runnin' right behind the sleigh—maybe twenty feet er so. The pack's leader had his head down, and his jaws were slaverin'. They didn't howl or make a sound, just kept comin' on. Now and then the leader would pull ahead, right beside the back runner, and look at me like a cannibal measures a missionary.

"If I hadn't left my rifle, everything would have been all right. I had nothin' to beat those beasts off with except my groceries—a few cans of peaches, beans, and peas. You can't kill a wolf with a can of peas that ain't much bigger than Number 9 shot. I tell you I was scairt. There's times when it's smart to be brave in the woods, and times when it's smarter to be scairt. Yes, sir!

"Pretty soon that old wolf leader, eyes sparkin' fire and tongue as red as a hot poker, slipped up to Mr. Bones and nipped his flank. Tore the flesh, he did. The blood maddened the pack. They swept round the sleigh on each side, leapin' and snappin' at Mr. Bones and Hatrack. Lots of pioneers have been set on by wolves, but this was my first attack. I had to do something quick or I'd lose my horses and my own life.

"In my excitement, I'd forgotten my pipe. An idea came to me." Plum Nelly got up from his chair and paced the floor. "I blew big smoke rings quicker than lightnin'. The rings froze solid in a second. I never worked so fast in my life. All the while the mad beasts were tearin' and snappin' at poor Mr. Bones and Hatrack. I hitched a length of rope to each ring. Leaning out, I tossed a ring over each wolf's head, collaring them tighter than Old Nick himself. Every last one of 'em, just as I'd planned, jerked back on the rope. I dragged 'em to death in less than half a mile. Towed 'em home that way, skinned the scoundrels, and collected a bounty come spring."

"Gee," said Sandy, "that's quite a story."

"I kin prove it, too. Uncle Bert saw me cut those ice collars off," Plum Nelly said, sitting down. "A homesteader had ter be self-reliant up here forty-odd years ago and get along with what he had; all I had was solidified smoke rings and a coil of hemp. There's a jug of cider in the cellar, Kit, if you want to get it."

"The cellar?" Kit said stupidly, not believing northern cabins had cellars. "Where's the cellar?"

"Where most cellars are," said Plum Nelly. "Under the house. What ails you today, Kit?"

"Nothin'," Kit said shortly. "How do you get down there?"

"Why," answered Plum Nelly, as if there were nothing to it, "all you do is lift that hide rug in the middle of the floor, pull up the trap door, and climb down a ladder."

The cellar that Plum Nelly had dug and lined with brick was as neat as any fussy housewife's. Along one wall stood cases of canned goods, the winter reserve that a man who lives alone in the north country lays by. Potato bins took up another wall, side by side with bins of sand in which Plum Nelly buried root vegetables. A molasses barrel swung in a wooden rocker, so that a slight tilt would start sweetening running from its applewood spout. Drying herbs, looking for all the world like useless weeds, hung from pegs—basil and marjoram and sage, and even lemon mint. Yellow onions filled one box, and white onions another. A brisket of beef soaked in an earthen jar. This was Plum Nelly's corned beef in the making. Kit saw a side of bacon, a ham, and a gallon of catsup. A sack of beans was flung on top of the flour barrel.

"Plum Nelly won't go hungry, will he?" Sandy said as he peeked through the trap door. "He's got everything."

"You're not kiddin'—everything but pickled pigs' feet," Kit laughed from below. "He's had enough of those for life. Here's the cider jug." He held the jug high as he climbed up the ladder.

"Ah," sighed Plum Nelly, swishing his drink a few minutes later, "there's nothing quite as good as cider—sweet cider pressed in a hand mill." The nut-brown liquid gurgled down his throat. "Ah!" he said again.

Sandy put down his cup and went to the window. The snow had stopped falling. Already it was covered with a crisscross of tracks—prints of squirrels going about their business, of chipmunks hurrying home, of sparrows swooping down to snatch at crumbs the boys had tossed out.

"Let's go for a walk, Kit," Sandy said.

Kit put on boots, and Sandy pulled the collar of his fleece-lined coat around his ears. When they stepped out, the cold caught at their throats, seeking to pull the breath from them. *Golly,* Sandy said to himself, *it's a lot colder than I thought.* He cupped mittened hands over mouth and nose.

Walking was easy in the fluffy whiteness, for this was not the heavy snow that comes in November to blanket

the north country until spring. Then only snowshoes can
carry a man on his round of chores and to the trap line.
But to the two boys it was a true storm, and for the first
time they saw the change that snow makes. Familiar land-
marks had mysteriously altered shape. The fishhouse was a
cotton puffball. The dock was a white enamel pathway
surrounded by the lake's deep blue. As the boys watched, a
large-mouth bass did a thunderous belly flop in the bay.

"Let's climb the hill," shouted Kit, jumping over a drift.
"No snowballing, now," he warned, seeing Sandy with his
arm drawn back. Sheepishly Sandy let the ball drop.

Climbing Plum Nelly's hill in soft snow was a puffing
job. The boys stopped to rest several times, but when they
finally reached the top they knew the exercise was worth
while.

"Will you just look at that?" breathed Kit.

Sandy only nodded, too out of breath to talk. Below
them stretched Broadwater Bay, a blue plate whose edges
were trimmed with green evergreens splashed with purest
white. Back from the lake stretched the dark forest. To
their right, smoke from Plum Nelly's chimney climbed to
the sky.

Sandy stepped out on the crest to see better. He looked
at the top of a tall dead pine. At first he thought the huge
white thing sitting there was just a mass of snow that
had somehow collected between trunk and branch. He
looked again, blinking. That wasn't snow.

"Kit," he whispered, pointing, "what's that?"

"Where?"

"Over there, in the top of that dead pine."

As Kit watched, the white object came to life, unfolding

wings that stretched farther than the boys had ever seen on a bird. It flapped away, silent as snowfall itself.

"Oh bro-*ther!*" cried Sandy. "Kit, what was it?"

Kit stood with his mouth open, and a chill that was not the weather crept up his spine. The great bird was like something out of an evil tale. When it had vanished, he could hardly believe that he'd seen it. It was too big, too white, too silent to be real. Yet Kit knew it lived.

"Was it a white eagle?" Sandy plucked at Kit's sleeve. "Was it, huh?" Sandy jumped up and down in excitement. "Is its nest in that tree?"

Kit shook his head. "Nope," he said with more confidence than he felt, "it's no eagle." He wished he were back in the warm safety of the cabin. "I don't know what it was, Sandy," he said gently. "Come on, let's ask Plum Nelly."

The boys burst into the cabin, not stopping to clean boots or shake snow from their clothes. They banged the door and stomped through the kitchen to the front room. Their father and Plum Nelly, table drawn in front of the roaring fire, were playing chess.

Plum Nelly was saying, "You'll lose your bishop, John, if you move that way," when the boys roared in.

"We saw a great big bird," panted Sandy, "and he—"

"—was sitting in the top of a dead pine," added Kit. "What was it?"

"Yah, Plum Nelly, what was it? Golly, he was big." Sandy whipped off his coat.

"Whoa, now. Take it easy. A big bird, you say? There are lots of big birds up here," said Plum Nelly. "What makes you fellows so excited?" Plum Nelly turned to the chess board. "How big was it?"

" 'Bout fifty feet across," cried Sandy. "Wasn't he, Kit?"

"Bigger than that," Kit said positively.

"This I have to hear," Plum Nelly said to Mr. Duncan. "We'll finish the game later. Now then, boys." Plum Nelly faced Kit and Sandy, warming themselves at the fire. "Suppose you tell me the truth. No bird up here has a fifty-foot wingspread. What did you see?"

Plum Nelly listened to the boys describe the creature— how it was white as snow, how it perched on a dead limb, and how it unfolded great wings to disappear. "It sure gave me a funny feeling," Kit confessed.

"Well," Plum Nelly said, making a tent of his hands, "I guess you really did see something. Yes, I reckon you did. And if you did, you saw one of the wonders of the north woods."

"But what was it?" insisted Kit.

"A snowy owl," Plum Nelly said quietly. "But he doesn't really belong down here. He lives on the islands of the far north. Every few years food gets scarce for the snowy owl. Then he travels south to fill his stomach."

"What do they eat?" asked Mr. Duncan, now as interested as everyone else.

"Mice and rats and sometimes rabbits and even muskrats. A hungry snowy owl will take chickens, ducks, and grouse," said Plum Nelly, "but he doesn't do much harm. Sometimes, when food is really scarce, they'll go right into the heart of a city, sitting on steeples and chimneys for days at a time. Then one day they'll disappear."

"They sure must eat a lot," said Sandy, "they're so big."

Plum Nelly chuckled. "They're big, all right, but the wingspread comes closer to fifty inches instead of fifty feet like you said. You fellows certainly tell tall tales. If you hadn't been so scared—" here Plum Nelly looked hard at the boys—"you'd have noticed the snowy owl has a blue-black beak, round yellow eyes, and polished black claws—"

"No wonder I thought it was the devil," said Kit. "You'd be scared, too, if you saw something that you'd never seen before, all white and mixed up with yellow beak and black eyes and—"

"You're gettin' everything mixed up and backwards," warned Plum Nelly, "including the colors. The Chippewa Indians thought the snowy owl brought good luck. Here you go talking about him as the devil. I'm right glad you saw him. Not too many do any more. There's no more beautiful bird in the whole north country, to my way of thinkin'."

"You say seeing a snowy owl brings good luck?" Kit asked.

"Sure did," Plum Nelly answered sagely.

"Oh bro-*ther!*" said Sandy, looking at Kit. "Am I glad I saw him first!"

"You don't need luck," Kit said. "You're the luckiest little guy I know."

Plum Nelly turned from the chess board. "Sandy sure does need luck," he said, " 'cause it's his turn to go for water."

"He who laughs last," snickered Kit, "laughs best."

Sandy grabbed the water bucket and fled.

8 *Uncle Bert Comes to Call*

While Sandy was pumping water, a car rattled up. When he came down the path, bucket sloshing, he saw an ancient truck standing in front of the cabin. *Now, that's queer,* he said to himself, shifting the pail from one hand to the other. A tank filled the truck's back end, rising to the top of the driver's cab. Sandy set the pail down and walked around the truck. There were no faucets on the tank, so he knew it couldn't be an oil truck. And anyway, Plum Nelly didn't use oil. The wind bit at the boy's ears, and he hurried into the cabin.

"Sandy," said Plum Nelly, waving toward a man who stood warming himself at the fireplace, "this is Uncle Bert. You've heard me talk about him."

"How do you do, sir," Sandy said in his most polite voice.

"Gladtuhmeetyuh," said the man, running words together so fast that Sandy thought at first he had sneezed.

Nobody said anything for a minute.

Finally Plum Nelly said, "That's Uncle Bert's minnow truck out front."

"Oh," Sandy answered. He put the bucket in place, wishing he knew what a minnow truck was, but he was ashamed to ask. He looked desperately around the room, knowing he should say something. The trouble was he didn't know what to say. Sandy glanced at his father, but Mr. Duncan was studying the chess board as calmly as if the stranger weren't there. Kit pretended to be finding fleas on Yellow Dog Dingo, although Dingo hadn't scratched since summer.

Sandy remembered what Plum Nelly had told him about Uncle Bert: how he was the nicest man and the handiest man in the whole county; how Uncle Bert could do almost anything with his hands—build a snug house, patch a roof, dig post holes, or lay a stone fireplace neater and prettier than a mason. Sandy saw that Uncle Bert was made Yankee-style—tall and lean, with crinkly blue eyes like Uncle Sam's, and with a quick speech that was like Uncle Sam's, too. All at once Sandy decided he liked Uncle Bert.

"What's a minnow truck?" he asked so suddenly that everyone laughed. Even Kit stopped searching for fleas.

"Well, bub," said Uncle Bert, with a little Down East in

his voice, "in the summertime I seine minnows to sell to resort owners who sell them to fishermen. That tank is my delivery wagon. I load the minnows in there and deliver them fresh as a daisy. Do pretty well at it, too. 'Course, this time of year, the tank's empty. I'll take it off pretty soon and start hauling wood."

"You mean you deliver bait just like the milkman delivers milk at home or the bakery truck brings bread?" Kit asked.

"Bub, that's it exactly—just exactly," Uncle Bert said.

Plum Nelly poured a cup of cider, then set the jug on the floor. "How about some cider, Uncle Bert? The boys here think it's all right, judgin' from the way the jug looks."

"I'll ride with the devil as long as he's going my way." Uncle Bert took the cup. He wiped his mouth, rubbing the back of a hand across his lips. "Not bad, not bad at all." He held out the cup, and Plum Nelly once more tilted the jug.

"Plum Nelly says you made his fireplace and put up the fence," said Kit, determined to talk as much as Sandy and show that he wasn't bashful.

"Bub, that's it exactly—just exactly." Uncle Bert's grin was friendly as a puppy's tail. "Had more trouble with the holes for the fence posts than I did with the fireplace, though."

"How's that?" Plum Nelly looked grave. "Why, I didn't know you did any frettin' 'bout my post holes. What happened?"

Uncle Bert considered, looking at Kit and Sandy as if perhaps they wouldn't understand fence trouble. "Oh, nothing much—just those dern muskrats." He swallowed his cider.

"What do you mean—muskrats?" Sandy couldn't see what muskrats had to do with post holes. Kit was puzzled, too.

"Well, to tell the truth, I wasn't going to say anything about it. Didn't want to upset you, Plum Nelly." Uncle Bert coughed, a little apologetic cough, but his lively blue eyes twinkled like candlelight.

"Get on with it," Plum Nelly said. Kit could see that Plum Nelly took pride in his place and worried when things went wrong.

"Now, don't get all lathered up." Uncle Bert eased into a chair. Sandy giggled, and got a stern look from his father. "You remember," continued Uncle Bert, "I worked till dark digging post holes. The next morning I went back to set the posts. There weren't any holes! First I thought maybe I'd missed the place where I'd dug. I was at the right spot, but the post holes were gone. Only thing I could do was dig another set. Next morning the second batch of holes was gone—clean disappeared."

"Great guns and pickled pigs' feet," roared Plum Nelly, shaking his finger under Uncle Bert's nose. "Holes don't disappear. Holes are holes." Plum Nelly turned to the boys. "Don't believe a word he says. Nobody can lose a hole, not even up here."

"Will you just let me finish?" begged Uncle Bert. "I hid in a thicket, where I had a good view of those holes. By hook or crook I was going to find out what was the matter. In about an hour what did I see but a big old muskrat with a yard-long beard as gray as pine ashes nosing along the holes. Behind him marched a row of rats. Each one picked out a nice post hole and carried it away. I followed. Well, sir, those rats carried them to the lake shore, dove down, and pushed every hole into the bank to use as nests. What do you think of that, boys?" Uncle Bert looked so hurt and perplexed by the whole business that Kit and Sandy burst into roars of laughter.

"So," said Plum Nelly, trying mighty hard to keep his face straight, "so that's what happened!"

"Yes, sir," Uncle Bert said vigorously, "and ever since then I always set muskrat traps when I dig post holes. Caught a hundred and seventeen of the rascals that way last fall, and never lost a hole!"

In the shouts that followed, Kit hefted a log onto the dying fire, careful to set it straight and true across the andirons. Sparks winged up like a swarm of bright summer insects. Kit watched the chimney swallow the brilliant reds, greens, and golds, then turned to Uncle Bert. "Know any more stories?" he asked.

"Reckon so," said the tall man, "but don't know if you'd like them."

"Sure, we'd like them." Sandy was as eager as Kit, and both boys came closer.

Uncle Bert stretched his long legs. He looked at Plum Nelly as if asking if it would be all right to spin more Yankee talk. Some signal the boys didn't see must have passed between the men, for Uncle Bert said he guessed he remembered a little thing that happened up near Cut Foot Sioux.

"Well," Uncle Bert began slowly, doing his brag-best, "I was camping with Lemon Drop Larsen, a big moose of a man who always carried a pocketful of lemon drops. That's how he got his name. Everybody in Cass County knew Lemon Drop. You remember him, don't you, Plum Nelly?"

Plum Nelly nodded. "Sure."

"I thought so." Uncle Bert was pleased. "Lemon Drop was so strong he lifted three-hundred-and-fifty-pound barrels of salt pork as if they were feathers, and hundred-and-eighty-pound sledges like matches. He was real big, he was. But he was clumsy and slow-witted. His size didn't help him when he got into the tightest spot in his life. And I was right there to see it."

"What happened?" asked Kit, poking the fire.

"All his life Lemon Drop wanted to kill a bear," said Uncle Bert, "—in spite of the fact that he couldn't hold a gun steady on anything. He couldn't hit the side of a mountain right in front of him even if his rifle was steadied in a vise. Nobody in camp understood why. They took Lemon Drop out for practice days at a time, standing him up in front of the target, showing him how to snuggle his cheek against the gun stock, and how to squeeze—not jerk —the trigger. Lemon Drop would work his candy under his tongue, close his eyes, and bang! He missed by a liar's mile. Every time he missed."

"Gosh!" Sandy said sadly, "that's too bad, 'specially if Lemon Drop wanted to kill a bear."

"Lemon Drop wanted to, all right, but he just couldn't get the hang of a gun. Awkward as a woman, he was." Uncle Bert chuckled. "Just couldn't learn, no matter how hard he tried. He blamed a wart on his trigger finger, saying it was bad luck. Well sir, everybody in camp told Lemon Drop how to get rid of that wart. You'd-a died. He rubbed that pesky wart with plug tobacco, and he dosed it with snuff. He tied a silk thread around it, thinking it would drop off. That didn't do any good. Finally an old Finn hit on the right magic.

"Lemon Drop rubbed his trigger-finger wart with an old dirty rag every day until full moon. He cursed the rag by bell, book, and candle. After dark, in bare feet and nightshirt, Lemon Drop buried the cloth behind the camp stable. Next morning the wart was gone. Poof! Like that, only quicker."

Kit opened his mouth, but Uncle Bert hurried on. "Lemon Drop's shooting wasn't any better without the wart than with it. The camp was plumb discouraged. He still couldn't hit the nose on his face even if he had been aiming at it—which, of course, he wasn't.

"Like most Swedes, Lemon Drop was a stubborn old goat. Without saying a word to the camp boss or any of the teamsters or even the timekeeper, one afternoon Lemon Drop took his rifle and slipped out of camp to get him a bear. He was clean out of lemon drops, so he carried a sack of cinnamon sticks. I wouldn't have known a thing about it except that I was cutting on top of Eagle Crest Ridge—back here a couple of miles—and saw Lemon Drop stumbling through the woods. He'd stop now and then, take a paper bag from his mackinaw, and pop a cinnamon stick in his mouth. Next thing I—"

"Say, Uncle Bert—" Kit broke in.

"What, bub?" Uncle Bert looked mighty annoyed.

"How did Lemon Drop get so much candy way up here in the woods?"

"Well, now, bub—umph—well, you see, it was this way."

Uncle Bert tugged at his collar as if the room were too warm. "Why," he continued, breathing a little fast, "Lemon Drop had a keg of lemon drops sent up with the supply wagon every two months. That's it exactly—just exactly. I remember now." Uncle Bert quit fiddling with his collar. Over in the corner, Plum Nelly grinned but kept quiet.

"Oh," Kit said doubtfully.

"Let's see, where was I?" Uncle Bert thought hard. "Oh, yes. Lemon Drop was stumbling through the woods, making more noise than a bull in a china shop. He'd just put his paper sack in his pocket when it happened."

"What happened?" This time it was Sandy who interrupted.

A great growl broke from Uncle Bert, sounding so much like an angry bear that Yellow Dog Dingo leaped to his feet. His lips curled and the hair on his back stood stiff.

"That's what happened," Uncle Bert said in a deep growly voice. "That's it exactly. One of the biggest bears I ever saw in the woods—a black monster—waddled out right in Lemon Drop's path! His little eyes were red-mad and he slavered and drooled. He was so big." Uncle Bert raised an arm over his head. "That tall he was—maybe taller. And must've weighed close to eight hundred pounds. There he was, walking on hind legs toward Lemon Drop with his massive arms out to crush and bear-hug him to death."

Yellow Dog Dingo lay down again but kept a wary eye on Uncle Bert, who talked like a man one minute and roared like a bear the next. To Dingo, Uncle Bert had to be either man or bear. The dog finally decided Uncle Bert

was a man, but a foolish one who perhaps thought he was a bear. Putting his nose on a paw, Dingo fell asleep. He had lived with human beings long enough not to be too surprised at anything they did.

"I sure thought," continued Uncle Bert, "that Lemon Drop was a goner. He fumbled his gun, the way he always did, and finally dropped it smack on the ground. The bear reared closer. Lemon Drop made a wild grab for his weapon, clutched it with butter fingers, and started to load. The bear came nearer. And nearer.

"Lemon Drop, with more luck than sense, slid a handful of shells in his rifle. The bear was clawing out for Lemon Drop when the charge hit. Point-blank range it was. I tell you, boys," beamed Uncle Bert, "I sure was tickled with Lemon Drop; for the first time in his life he'd hit something with a gun.

"But the bear didn't fall dead the way it ought to. It roared twice as hard as before, dropped on all fours, and scuttled away through the woods. I saw it all from up there on top of the ridge. Lemon Drop watched the bear go, and began to shake. He held on to a pine to keep from falling down, and shook so hard he shook every last needle off the tree! Pretty soon he eases back to camp, being mighty careful to meet nobody."

"But Uncle Bert," Kit said, "if Lemon Drop hit the bear, why didn't it die?"

"Yeh," said Sandy, "I thought of that, too. Why didn't he, Uncle Bert?"

Uncle Bert, his honest Yankee face drawn up solemn-like, thought hard. "I guess there's no harm in telling you now; after all, Lemon Drop's been gone a long time. You see, fellows, Lemon Drop was so rattled when he loaded his rifle that he pushed in a handful of cinnamon sticks instead of bullets. He shot that bear with candy! Yes, sir, he just filled that black bear's hide with cinnamon. That's it— that's it exactly!"

Uncle Bert got his coat and overshoes. "Time for me to be getting along."

"Better tell the rest of it before you go," suggested Plum Nelly mildly.

"Well . . ." Uncle Bert hesitated, his hand on the door latch. "Promise you won't tell?" he said to the boys. They nodded.

"Okay," said Uncle Bert. "Next year, for the first time, cinnamon bear cubs appeared in America. Cute little fellows they were, too."

"Hey! Wait a minute!" Kit called. "Cinnamon bears don't live up here. My science book says they live down south. Now, what about that?"

"Shucks," said Uncle Bert, halfway through the door, "that's easy. They left here because it was too cold for cinnamon bears!"

The door slammed, and soon the boys heard Uncle Bert's minnow truck rattle into life. A horn squawked, loud and insistent. Sandy stuck his head out in time to hear Uncle Bert call cheerfully, "That's it—that's it *exactly!*"

9 The Magic Tackle Box

"Now here," said Plum Nelly proudly, "is a mighty unusual tackle box. It's magic."

The box, square and sturdy, looked to Kit and Sandy like a million others. It was battered and scratched, and the handle was mended with tape. Three trays held Plum Nelly's gear—spoon hooks honed to razor sharpness, tiny fishing flies cunningly tied with orange floss and fashioned from the dark fur of a hare's ear spun on primrose silk, and huge, evil daredevils for the catching of pickerel. There was a casting reel and a spinning reel. There were lifelike plastic crickets and crawfish and dragonflies, and even red ants and baby grubs. The magic tackle box held June bugs of gold and silver, and green rubber frogs whose legs wiggled and swam. Small jars of colored pork rind, packets of leader nylon, lead sinkers, safety pins—all these and more filled the trays and spilled over.

"Umph," Kit grunted, pointing to the tangle of lures and baits, "the only magic about this box is that it would take a magician to find anything in it!"

Plum Nelly snapped the lid shut so quickly that Kit had to jerk his hand away. "Don't be too wise, young feller," said Plum Nelly, "or I won't take you with me."

"Where you going, Plum Nelly?" Sandy trotted along with the guide, trying to talk and eat a peanut butter sandwich at the same time.

"Me and my magic tackle box," said Plum Nelly, "are going to Leech Lake, and there we're going to catch pike till who laid the chunk."

"Till who laid the chunk?"

"Yup," said Plum Nelly shortly, "till who laid the chunk!"

Sandy trotted off, clutching his half-eaten sandwich and repeating under his breath, "Till who laid the chunk, till who laid the chunk, till who laid the chunk!" He was so busy muttering that he ran smack-bang into his father coming down the path.

"Whoa there, son! What's the rush?"

"Say, Dad," said Sandy, waving a peanut-smeared crust excitedly, "what does 'who laid the chunk' mean, huh?"

"Why, that's easy. It's a slang saying that means a lot of

anything. If I told you, Sandy, that you ate peanut butter sandwiches 'till who laid the chunk,' I'd mean that you put down an awful lot of peanut butter sandwiches. What do you want to know for?" Mr. Duncan started down the path with Yellow Dog Dingo at his heels.

"Well," said Sandy, giving Dingo the last of his sandwich, "Plum Nelly says he's going to Leech Lake and catch fish till who laid the chunk!"

"So this is the day for the Leech Lake trip." Mr. Duncan turned abruptly to Sandy. "Where's Plum Nelly now?"

"Last I saw of him he was heading for the barn with his magic tackle box. Pop, is that box really magic?"

Sandy looked so serious that his father grinned. "Guess it is, son. Anyway, Plum Nelly catches an awful lot of fish with the stuff he's got in that box. There he is now. Hey, Plum Nelly! I hear we're going over to Leech."

"Great guns and pickled pigs' feet," shouted Plum Nelly, "who told you? Yep, we're goin', all right. Kit's down at the boathouse now gettin' some things I sent him for. Put yer stuff in the jeep, and we'll take off in thirty minutes. And Sandy—"

"Yes, sir?"

"We're goin' to catch fish till who laid the chunk!"

"You bet," Sandy grinned. "Till who laid the chunk!"

"Stop it!" cried Kit, coming up with his arms full of life jackets. "You two quit jawing about that chunk layer and help me load the jeep. Plum Nelly's in a hurry."

Plum Nelly nodded, turned, and entered the barn. The boys heard him hammering and banging and making more noise than a steam drill going through cement. Plum Nelly stuck his head out of the door. "You fellers can't go until you find today's treasure!"

"I've got the slip right here." Kit dug deep in faded jeans—his lucky jeans, he called them, for everything always went all right when he wore them. This paper, unlike others, was plain and to the point.

One look, and the boys whooped across the snow and into the minnow house. "It says to look behind the first shelf on the right," panted Kit, fumbling off his mittens. Sandy stumbled over Yellow Dog Dingo and fell flat. Kit hauled him up roughly. "Can't you ever stay on your feet?" he hissed.

"That's the shelf." Sandy pointed and reached out a hand. Kit, still cross, batted Sandy's hand away. "Here, let me," he said, thrusting his fingers far to the back of the pine board. He pulled out two small packages done up in brown wrapping paper.

"Give me one—one is mine!" Sandy jumped up and down in excitement, took a backward step, tripped over Dingo, and fell down again. Dingo howled and shot out of the minnow house, yelling all the way to the barn, although he hadn't been really hurt.

Kit thrust a package at Sandy. "Here, stumblebum. For Pete's sake, try to stay on your feet. What's the matter with you today, anyway? You can't fall all over yourself at Leech Lake or you'll plop overboard."

But Sandy was too busy tearing off wrappings to pay attention to his brother's ill-humor. Kit sighed. Sometimes having a younger brother was more bother than the measles.

"Lookit!" Sandy held up a shiny metal case.

Kit nodded. "I've got one, too, but what is it?"

"It's a handwarmer," cried Sandy, proud he knew something Kit didn't. "You fill it with fluid like Dad does his cigarette lighter. Gosh! It stays warm for hours and it won't burn your hands or clothes. Oh bro-*ther!*"

Plum Nelly saw them coming, two boys with faces beaming, their new-found treasure bright in the rays of the after-storm sun. "It's a wonderful America," he said to Mr. Duncan, "when youngsters are free to love the woods."

The jeep, Mr. Duncan said later, looked like a gypsy's wagon. Plum Nelly had kept the boys busy carrying and packing until Kit, exhausted, said, "I never knew so much stuff went on a fishing trip."

Once the jeep got under way, Kit forgot aching muscles in the autumn beauty of the Woodtick Trail. The October sun, riding high and red, melted yesterday's snowfall, just as Uncle Bert had predicted. Patches of white still clung to emerald evergreens, but the trail was clean enough. Sometimes early snow in the north country disappears as rapidly as it comes. This was one of those days.

Plum Nelly, a knitted cap atop his head, drove with one hand, pointed with the other, and kept up a steady chatter. "There's a fire warden's tower!" The jeep bucked like a bronco. "Got a deer right in that cutover patch last year." He drove straight through a mudhole, the splash not bothering him at all. "You ought ter see Woodtick in the dead of winter. Six feet of snow make a lot of difference the way things look." Plum Nelly wheeled round a thank-you-ma'am. "Lookit that snowshoe jump!" he shouted. The boys looked and saw nothing. Plum Nelly grinned wide as a watermelon slice. "You got ter be quick. Those bunnies sure make time."

Sandy grabbed the lunch box as the jeep swerved around another curve, hit pavement, and straightened out, Kit said later, like a footballer making fifty yards for a touchdown in nothing flat. Mr. Duncan jerked his hat down to keep it from sailing away. Nobody was prepared for what happened next. Without slowing, Plum Nelly yanked the jeep into a dirt road, stepped on the gas, and scooted along as if Old Nick himself was right behind. Then, just as quickly, he slammed on the brakes, tumbling boys, luggage, and lunch together in a confused pile.

They stopped along a gravel beach that touched an ocean of sparkling blue, dotted here and there with islands whose trees showed against the horizon like weary sentinels. "This is Sugar Point," Plum Nelly said in his best show-off manner, "and that's Leech Lake. It's forty miles across, some places, and has more than six hundred miles of shore line. Right here"—and Plum Nelly gestured dramatically—"an Indian battle was fought." He dug a boot into the sand. "Use ter find arrowheads and sich."

A lake wind, riding miles of chilled whitecaps, stung faces and watered the boys' eyes. Sandy pulled his mackinaw closer. Under it the softness of his new buckskin shirt helped turn the wind. "It's going to be cold out there in a boat," he said.

"You bet it is." Plum Nelly scrambled into the jeep and roared the motor. "Come on, we haven't got all day."

Twenty minutes later Kit and Sandy were carrying rods and duffel from the jeep to Boots' launch that lay harbor-snug in a small cove. Boots was Uncle Bert's son, a boy much like his father, with the same quick speech and the same blue eyes that crinkled and laughed. His launch, with inboard motor throbbing when the jeep skidded up, was not long and slick and fancy, like a thoroughbred racer, but short and stubby and strong, like a work horse. Below deck a tiny cabin held two bunks and a table. Screwed to the aft deck were fishing chairs.

Kit handed tackle boxes, life jackets, and extra coats and sweaters over the launch's rail to Sandy. Plum Nelly wouldn't let the boys touch the magic tackle box. Only when all was stowed neatly and the boat headed through the narrows into choppy water did Sandy have a chance to rest. He flopped into a fishing chair, feeling the deck rise and fall under him as the launch plowed steadily for Pelican Island. The wind rose and spray splashed over the rail. Kit lurched up from below in oilskins and rain hat. "Pop says you're to get into some of these," he shouted. Sandy nodded, hanging on to his chair for dear life as the launch shook itself loose from a wave.

When Sandy slid into the cabin, Mr. Duncan and Plum Nelly were filling coffee cups from a gallon Thermos jug and eating great sandwiches of corned beef. "Want a sandwich?" Plum Nelly asked. Sandy shook his head. Suddenly he felt a little queer: the air was hot down here, and he didn't want anything to eat at all. He didn't even want to smell food. Plum Nelly saw him gulp and his cheeks go pale. "Hey!" he shouted. "None of that, lad. This isn't rough. Take your slicker and hop on deck where the air's fresh. Scram! You'll git yer sea legs soon enough. But stay in the air till you do! We'll be fishing mighty soon."

Sandy grabbed a rainsuit and staggered up on deck, clinging to a rail that swooped up and down. *I won't get sick*, he kept saying to himself, *I won't get seasick on a lake!* But his face was so green that Boots, swaying easy-like at the wheel, spoke sharply. "Stick yer face into the wind, bub!" He sounded for all the world like Uncle Bert, talking fast and through his nose. "Don't look at the water. Look up! You're not the first to feel squeamish on Leech. It'll pass."

Boots' comforting words reassured Sandy. Before long he was better. Color stole back into his cheeks, he didn't feel clammy, and he found the launch's pitch fun. He tried a long breath. Yep, everything stayed down!

Boots pointed ahead, over the spray-soaked prow. "Yonder's the fishing fleet." A string of boats, perhaps half a hundred, circled off the shore of Pelican Island. A launch or two moved in the procession, but most were outboards, bobbing in the wind. Boots cut his speed, watched his chance, and skillfully took his place in the circle. Every boat had lines out, and almost every boat dragged strings heavy with walleyes.

A hand fell on Sandy's shoulder. "Now," said Plum Nelly, "here's how we rig for pike." He fixed a heavy weight to his line and tied on a long nylon leader. A June-bug spinner was fastened to the leader. On the spinner's hook Plum Nelly threaded a live shiner minnow, running the hook through the minnow's mouth, out the gill, and under and through the fin. "Now then," Plum Nelly said, "we're ready." He threw the line overboard, letting a hundred feet sing out, and then held the trolling rod steady.

Kit got mixed up putting on a minnow, but Sandy was ready soon after Plum Nelly. He felt the spinner working in the water far behind the launch's wash. Sandy wiggled into a fishing chair, braced his feet, and hoped he'd get a strike. He and Plum Nelly fished one side of the launch, and Kit and his father the other.

Something tapped Sandy's bait, stopped, and then— *wham!* "Strike and fish," yelled Plum Nelly, pulling his line out of Sandy's way. "Stay with him, son! He's a beaut! Don't horse him in too fast. That's the boy—easy does it! Whoop! Give him a little line. Great guns and pickled pigs' feet, don't get him fouled with the propeller." Sandy followed Plum Nelly's directions. "He's comin' in," shouted Plum Nelly. "Oh, Moses, Moses, don't give him slack. Steady now!" Plum Nelly's landing net made a beautiful sweep under the water. A marvelously quick turn of the wrist, and a great fish with bulging opal eyes flopped on deck. "It'll go five pounds if it's an ounce," gloated Plum Nelly. "Hurrah for Sandy—cham-pi-on fisherman!"

All morning the walleyes came in, first on Mr. Duncan's line, then on Kit's and Plum Nelly's and Sandy's. They filled a stringer and put a second overboard. Boots, steering with one hand and fishing with the other, filled his limit. The hungry walleyes were striking normally—first a nibble, then another to mouth the bait, and then the sharp bite on the hook. And then the fun!

Fishing was wonderful, and then suddenly it was terrible. "Haul in your lines," Boots told the boys. "The fishing's over!"

"Why?" Kit asked.

Plum Nelly heard the question. "In the first place," he said, "walleyed pike feed best in early morning and late evening. It's noon now. In the second place, when they stop biting, they stop—right then. Nobody really knows why. They just stop, all of them, all at once." Plum Nelly rubbed his stomach. "The fish aren't hungry, but I am. Take 'er over to the island, Boots," he called, "and we'll have a picnic lunch."

Boots touched his cap. "Aye, aye, sir," he said, smart as any sailor. "I'll take her in off Mosquito Point."

The lunch was fit for a king—ham sandwiches, the bread cut thick as a man's thumb; baked beans that tantalized the boys with their smell of pork chunks and molasses; potato chips whose salt sent Sandy again and again to the water jug; and, best of all, fillets of fresh-caught pike, fried in fat over a driftwood fire. Cookies and chocolate bars finished the meal for Kit and Sandy. The men, hunkered down in the sand close to the fire, lit their pipes. Boots pulled a blanket over him and went to sleep as quickly and quietly as if he were home in bed. Where the fishing fleet had been, not a single boat remained. Leech Lake, as far as eye could see, showed only whitecaps chasing blue waves.

Plum Nelly yawned and reached for the coffee. "We'll troll a spell this afternoon on the way home, but don't hope fer much. Way I figure it, fishin' is over, except, of course, fer what I kin coax up from my magic box. Hop to it, Kit, and throw a small chunk on the fire." Plum Nelly stirred his coffee with a green twig. "Don't want too big a fire or we can't git close enough. Big, roarin' fires ain't worth their salt except in a girls' camp—an' girls don't know nothin'. A leetle fire 'bout so big"—Plum Nelly spread his hands—"kin warm a man and cook his victuals all ter once."

Mr. Duncan agreed, then asked, "Why is this called Mosquito Point, Plum Nelly?"

"Oh," said Plum Nelly, filling his coffee cup for the fifth time, "that's quite a yarn."

Sandy, eyes drowsy, hitched himself to the shelter of a half-buried log whose branches clawed through sand like wizened hands. If Plum Nelly was going to tell another story, he might as well be comfortable. Kit squatted by the fire he tended, drawing beach pictures with a pointed stick and, now and again, tossing driftwood to the flames.

A match rasped against cloth, burst into bright flame, and, in cupped hands, was held to blackened pipe bowl. Plum Nelly blew it out, carefully broke the match stick in two as every good woodsman does, and threw it away. "Now then, about how Mosquito Point got its name. Long, long ago, when men first walked this north country, everything was good. There was lots of deer and moose and fish, and always a lot of rice in the fall. Men were good to each other then, so there wasn't any reason to have pesky things around to punish them. Everybody ate good and was happy.

"But in the band of Indians who lived on Pelican Island was a medicine man who was very bad, and because he was so bad the chief men decided to banish him and make him wander forever through the woods alone.

"When the chief told the medicine man about this, he got madder than a sidewinder serpent and said, 'If you do this to me, I'll plague you and your sons and your women as long as I live.' This scared the chiefs a lot, and they left the evil maker of medicine alone. So he strutted around camp acting more important and more pesky than ever. He stole meat from his brothers' traps and wouldn't help with the rice harvest. When the Harvest Moon came, he was too lazy to build his own winter home, so when snow fell deep and the wind blew he moved into the lodge of one of the chiefs. There he ate what that brave man hunted. The chief was scared of the medicine man and there was nothing he could do about it.

"The evil medicine man spent the long winter living in turn with each of the chiefs. But when the thaws came and Leech Lake turned slate-dark, the chiefs met in council. They decided to kill the medicine man."

Kit flung another stick on the fire, and Sandy, his drowsy eyes now bright, moved closer. "Now, in those days," went on Plum Nelly, "all men were good, and nobody had ever killed his brother before, and the chiefs were afraid of what might happen to them. They were afraid the spirit of the medicine man would hang around camp and bring them bad luck.

"One chief said, 'We will bury him without a house, that his spirit may not linger here.'

"Another added, 'We will leave no food or knife with the body.'

"And a third said, 'We will burn him, that his spirit will lose its home completely.'

"And this is what they did. When they told him what they were going to do, the medicine man was scared and mad. First he threatened them; then he begged them not to kill him, but he could not change the minds of the chiefs. They were sure they had beaten him at last, and they weren't scared any more.

"As they bound the medicine man's hands and feet with hide, he said, 'I'll put a curse on the whole tribe of men. Never will you forget what you have done to me. Every year I will torture you for four moons. You will not escape my arrows until first frost. And in the warm moons you will never know peace.'

"But the chiefs just laughed at the medicine man, and they bound him to a stake and burned him. Before he died the medicine man cursed them, saying, 'You will never forget me.' But the chiefs just laughed. They were sure no harm could come to them. For hours they burned the body, poking the fire with hunting spears till there was nothing left but a heap of soft white ashes.

"The chiefs were happy. They danced round and round the heap of ashes that had been their enemy. Then—all of a sudden—a strong wind blew up out of the east. With a *poof* it hit the little white ashes, scattering them high in the air, and all around was a loud buzzing. The chiefs screamed in pain and slapped at their bare backs and faces. Each little ash was a tiny arrow, and each made a buzzing sound.

"And from that day to this, when the wind is from the east in the spring, the white ashes buzz and sting with their tiny arrows, for that is the day mosquitoes began. And this is the point where the Indians camped and where the chiefs burned the medicine man."

Kit stood up, face flushed from tending fire. "Is that a true story?"

Plum Nelly hesitated, then spoke quietly. "Yes, I think it's true enough. The Indians believed it to be true. Legends sometimes hold more truth than we suspect." He shrugged, looked at the lake which had quieted in the past hour, got up and walked over to Boots and shook him awake. "Time to leave Mosquito Point," he said, "if we're to get in some late trollin' and be home 'fore sundown."

Once aboard, with gear stowed snugly and all lines searching bottom water for pike, Plum Nelly opened his magic tackle box. One after another he held up favorite baits—Prescott spinners, Paul Bunyan deep trollers, Hawaiian wigglers. "Here," he told Sandy, "use the Prescott with the biggest shiner in the pail. Just for fun, I'm tryin' a deep diver."

Boots slowed to a snail's pace, zigzagging over rocky bottom and across deep-sunk sand bars. Kit soon tired of trolling and climbed up to stand beside Boots at the wheel. Mr. Duncan went below for a nap. Only Plum Nelly and Sandy fished, one from starboard and the other from port.

"Your magic fishing box isn't lucky this afternoon," said Sandy, cleaning green weeds from his hook.

Plum Nelly paid no attention. Sandy thought Plum Nelly hadn't heard, and then he saw the guide rear back and strike hard. "I got him! The devil's been fiddlin' fer five minutes an' finally took it. Wow!" Plum Nelly's line ripped from reel, singing the song of a big fish. The steel rod bent almost double. "That's no walleye," Plum Nelly grunted. "That's a northern."

Inch by inch Plum Nelly gained line, only to have it stolen away in swift runs. Sandy had never seen such a battle. He forgot his own pole in the excitement. Then, fifty feet behind the launch, a great shape broke water, jumping high in the air. Plum Nelly set his teeth and yanked. The northern crashed on the surface and dove deep. "Watch him, boy—there's a fish," said Plum Nelly, winning line.

Like all northerns, this one was a fighter. He sulked and rushed and broke water twice more before weakening.

Thirty minutes later, Plum Nelly led him to the launch's side and sunk a gaff under his chin. A quick heave, and the biggest fish Sandy had ever seen lay gasping on deck, its mammoth mouth open to show rows of wicked teeth. Plum Nelly got out tapeline and scales. "A yard and four inches, and twenty-two pounds," he said, "and you tell me my magic box is no good!"

Sandy was opening his mouth to apologize when the click of his reel sounded off in angry taps like an alarm ticker in a firehouse. He felt a heavy weight in the water. The weight hung dead, as if he had snared a boulder.

No matter how hard he tried, Sandy couldn't gain an inch of line. Plum Nelly laid a hand briefly on Sandy's rod, then called, "Slow her down, Boots; Sandy's got the bottom of the lake or the biggest fish we've seen all day." Plum Nelly turned to Sandy. "Great big fish sometimes act just like this. Now, take 'er easy and reel slow." Sandy did as he was told. Little by little his reel filled, but he felt no fight in the object he was so gradually lifting to the surface. Plum Nelly was leaning so far over the port rail that Sandy feared he'd go overboard.

Turn and reel. Reel and turn. Sandy thought he had been reeling forever when Plum Nelly cried, "That's no fish, but what in tarnation is it? A little more, Sandy. Great guns and pickled pigs' feet! Stop! I can reach it." Plum Nelly's arm went over the side and into the water. It came up, and something went bang! on the deck.

"There's yer fish!" shouted Plum Nelly.

"But . . . but what is it?" Sandy couldn't tell what the thing was. He looked again. "Why, it . . . why, it looks like a tomahawk!"

"It's a war ax all right," said Plum Nelly, "an' a good one. Chippewa, most likely, but mebbe Sioux." He untangled Sandy's fishing line. The polished stone was almost ten inches long, and had been fashioned and chipped by hands long since gone to the Happy Hunting Ground. "See," said Plum Nelly, "here's the groove where the handle fitted." He wiped the weapon dry and handed it to Sandy.

Even Kit, who frequently made fun of Sandy and sometimes thought secretly that young brothers were pests, was impressed by Sandy's Indian hatchet. "I'll bet you," he boasted, "not another guy in our school has a real Injun hatchet. Betcha not one guy in a hundred million million ever caught a war ax fishing. You're a pretty good kid, do you know it?"

Sandy paid little attention to his brother's praise, although ordinarily he would have been tickled to pieces. He was thinking hard, wondering how long his Indian ax had lain among the rocks of the lake bottom. Who had patiently chipped the stone? What Indian had laced a handle to it with rawhide? How did the ax get into the lake? These and a hundred more questions chased through his head.

Questions about the ax pecked at Sandy's mind all the long way back to Boots' dock. As soon as the launch was made fast, Sandy jumped over the side. He hurried to the jeep and carefully packed the Indian weapon in a burlap sack. He put the sack on the front seat. The ride home was made in swift-falling darkness. When Plum Nelly switched on headlights, a long gray shape that was loping along blurred into the shadows. "That was a wolf," said Plum Nelly.

A long day of fresh air and excitement made Sandy sleepy, but he tried hard to stay awake. He thought of the fun of trolling for walleyes and catching, instead, a real Indian hatchet. He'd sure put one over on Kit. Sandy's eyes drooped. An owl's mournful hoot was the last thing he heard. His head fell forward and his hand slipped from the burlap that held the war hatchet.

Yellow Dog Dingo heard Plum Nelly turn into the driveway and set up a thunderous baying. Sandy jerked awake and felt for his precious ax. The question that fretted him most tumbled out. "Plum Nelly, do you suppose my ax could've belonged to the Injuns who burned the bad medicine man?"

"Sure could," Plum Nelly answered, guiding Sandy into the cabin. "You better turn in. We'll tend to unloadin'."

A pleased smile lit Sandy's face. He trotted into the bunkroom on sleepy, staggering feet. When his father peeked in a few minutes later, Sandy was already in bed. He hadn't even bothered to hang up his clothes. But on the pillow, close to his tousled head, lay the ax. The boy looked up and mumbled, "We sure fished till who laid the chunk, didn't we, Dad?"

"We sure did," said Mr. Duncan, and closed the door.

10 How the Mississippi Came to Be

Sandy was sick. His nose ran and his throat hurt. Mr. Duncan said he had a bad cold, but Plum Nelly allowed it was the pip and wouldn't amount to a hill of beans if Sandy stayed home, kept warm, and drank a lot of hot stuff.

"There's jest no sense pamperin' the boy," snorted Plum Nelly, seeing Mr. Duncan fussing around with pills and a fever thermometer. "Treat a cold and it lasts two weeks; don't do nothin' an' it lasts a fortnight. It's six of one and half dozen of the other. Anyways—" Plum Nelly looked sternly at Sandy—"nobody stays sick long up here—the air cures anything."

"Well, the air better get to work mighty quick," snapped Mr. Duncan, shaking down the thermometer. "I guess he got chilled on Leech Lake the other day."

Sandy sneezed, a great blast that started as a nose tickle and ended with an explosion sharp as a two-bit cannon cracker on the Fourth of July. The sneeze was so loud that it startled Yellow Dog Dingo, who was napping on his back with his paws in the air.

"For Pete's sake," said Kit disgustedly; "he would have to go and get sick and spoil our vacation."

A muffled voice came out of Sandy. "I'm not sick. I dod a dold!"

"You sure have, son." Mr. Duncan slipped the thermometer into its case. "Plum Nelly's fine northern climate isn't going to cure you, either."

"That shows how much you know about it," yelped Plum Nelly, fairly dancing in anger. "Just let me tell you something, John Duncan. You don't know a blasted thing about our weather up here. It's better than any horse liniment ever concocted. Why, do you know I saw the weather cure something the doctors couldn't help? Do you?"

"No," said Mr. Duncan, "I don't."

"Saw it with my own eyes," went on Plum Nelly. "Yes, sir, with my own eyes. There wuz a smart salesman from over to Wisconsin come to Cass County to peddle plows an' harrows and sich. He wuz demonstratin' a reaper at the fair grounds. He got so derned excited he fell in front of the machine. The sickle, quicker than scat, cut off both of his legs and head, then the mules kicked his body halfway round the field. He was hurt bad—"

"Did he live?" Kit asked.

"Did he live?" Plum Nelly cast eyes to heaven. "Of course he lived! We just stuck his legs back on and set his head in place an' he wuz good as new. That is, he was all right as long as he stayed in Minnesota. But that night he started back to Wisconsin. Everything went fine until his buggy crossed the state line. Ten seconds after that he died and fell apart all over again. That's how healthy our climate is!"

"I suppose that's why Sandy doesn't have to worry about his cold," Mr. Duncan said dryly.

Plum Nelly spread his hands. "Isn't that what I've been sayin'? Now, John, you and Kit light out fer somewhere. I'll care fer Sandy. He's goin' ter be here when you git back. Aren't you, Sandy?"

Sandy nodded.

Mr. Duncan and Kit were no sooner out the door heading for Pew's Point than Plum Nelly, with an air of mystery, scuttled down the trap door to the cellar. Sandy heard him banging boxes and muttering to himself. He wondered what Plum Nelly was after and why he stayed so long. The kitchen, for all its coziness, was lonely with everybody gone. The clock ticked louder and louder. Sandy had a good notion to get out of his chair and see what Plum Nelly was doing, but the blanket around him was warm and he didn't feel like moving. He closed his eyes.

When he opened them Plum Nelly was busy at the stove. The kitchen smelled as good as a candy store and a popcorn wagon rolled into one. Sandy's nose followed the smell to the stove, where Plum Nelly was stirring a kettle. But he was too sleepy to ask Plum Nelly what he was mixing.

Sandy dozed again, dreaming fitfully as the fever ate into him. He saw the lid of Plum Nelly's magic tackle box pop open, and out of it flapped the snowy owl with its cruel beak tight in Yellow Dog Dingo's back. Dingo screamed, but the bird carried him high to a treetop. Sandy picked up his glass rod to kill the owl, but the rod melted into a tiny stick. The owl laughed and began to eat Dingo— Dingo was on a platter all covered with gravy, and the owl was carving him with a great knife and saying politely, "White or dark meat, Sandy?" "I won't eat Dingo," Sandy sobbed and fell out of the tree.

Sandy, bewildered and teary-eyed, woke to find Plum Nelly shaking him. "Great guns and pickled pigs' feet!" Plum Nelly tucked the blanket around Sandy. "Who asked you to eat Dingo, eh? You've been a-dreamin'! I've got something better for you than Dingo." He handed Sandy a bowl of a delicious-smelling soup, curving the boy's fingers around it and holding it to his lips. At first the steaming broth went down in dainty sips. Then Sandy gulped. When the bowl was empty, he lay back in his chair. The broth made him feel better. His bones didn't ache, and his head didn't hurt, and his sore throat wasn't as sore. Sandy felt all peaceful-like, with perhaps a part of him in Plum Nelly's comfortable kitchen and a part of him somewhere else.

Sandy considered napping again, but he forced his eyes open. "How did you make that soup, Plum Nelly? I feel better all the time."

"Shucks," said Plum Nelly, rinsing out the bowl, "it's an Indian remedy that the white men learned long ago. The lumberjacks used it, and the trappers before them made it. It's the best thing I know fer the pip, like you got." He dragged a stool beside Sandy's chair. "It's got healin' herbs in it—'yarbs,' my granddaddy called 'em in Ohio. He was a healer, and blended pennyroyal and strawberry leaves and rhubarb and even peppermint. Your broth—" Plum Nelly grinned broadly—"had ground-up poplar bark in it an' some prickly ash and black pepper and cinnamon an' . . . oh, a lot of other—"

"Oh bro-*ther!*" Sandy sat up straight. "You gave me real pioneer medicine?"

"Sure did," Plum Nelly said uneasily, "but mebbe yuh better not say anything to your dad 'bout the bark and powdered leaves and sich. He thinks a pill made in some glue factory is medicine." Plum Nelly snorted. "That stuff he gave you this mornin' wouldn't cure you in a month of Sundays. That's why I sent him away, so as to git you on your feet again. You're feeling better, aren't you?" Plum Nelly looked anxiously at Sandy.

"Yup." Sandy mopped his face.

"That's the fever breakin' up," said Plum Nelly. "You'll be fit as a fiddle come evenin'."

"Gee," said Sandy, "that's fine. Thanks, Doc Plum Nelly, thanks a lot."

Plum Nelly shrugged off Sandy's praise. "Nobody gains in weight from sweet words," he said. "Yep, your dad's got too blamed civilized, dependin' on gelatin pills an' vitamin pills, and pills fer this and pills fer that. Take I-yaw-shaw-way-ge-zhick, the Indian who—"

"What?" Sandy said. "Who did you say?"

Plum Nelly pulled his ear. "That's the name of the Indian who told me how to make the brew I gave you. I-yaw-shaw-way-ge-zhick means Crossing Sky."

"You're not fooling?"

"No, it's a real name. Crossing Sky spent a winter with me. Matter of fact, he taught me most all I know of trapping and setting a snare. He told me how the Mississippi was discovered, too."

"Oh, I read about that in school." Sandy was eager to make a good impression. "A fellow named Henry Schoolcraft discovered the Mississippi." The boy puzzled a minute. "I mean, he found where the river started—at Lake Itasca."

"Mebbe so," said Plum Nelly, "but I wasn't talkin' about that. Didn't they teach you in school about Father Water?"

Sandy shook his head.

"I declare," said Plum Nelly. "Well, Crossing Sky told it like this. A long time ago, before the white man came to America, Indians lived in peace. They believed in many spirits. Some were smaller than a gnat, others were as large and mean as a deer fly, and a few were big as the giant bellowing moose. All these spirits lived in the Land of Look-Behind, a sacred place known only to the medicine men.

"Their home was called the Land of Look-Behind because the tiny spirits and the medium-sized spirits and the spirits big as the lordly moose always sneaked up behind a man. Crossing Sky said his people tried walking backward so as to see the spirits that buzzed and stung and bit and drew blood. But no matter which way a warrior walked, the spirits were always behind.

"The tribe tried many ways to fool the spirits. Fearless hunters, with an eagle feather for bravery in their hair, wore horrible masks on the backs of their heads so the spirits wouldn't be able to tell whether a man was goin' forward or backward. They were the Two-Facers."

Sandy said eagerly, "Did that work, Plum Nelly?"

"Nope. Crossing Sky said the Two-Facers only made things worse. The spirits knew a warrior's real face and whether he was really goin' forward or not. They put a special curse on two-faced men, so that even today no one trusts them.

"Then the medicine men had a great pow-talk around the council fire. They built the fire of pine hearts and kindled it with the youngest flame struck from sacred flint. They sprinkled the infant blaze with tobacco, and fed the fire with the eyes of the lynx, the tail of the beaver, and the brain of the fox so as to see clearly, be strong, and think cunningly.

"The smoke hazed up and billowed out and grew into a cloud that tented the medicine men, shuttin' them away from the world. They were afraid. Out of the cloud came the Father Water—a giant who was sad and gentle and so big not one of the medicine men ever saw all of him. His voice, soft as whisperin' wind, told the awe-struck Indians crouched there around the fire not to fear the spirits of the Land of Look-Behind.

"Father Water told the medicine men he would trap the evil spirits from the Land of Look-Behind. From his own body he would scatter lakes the length and width of the north country, and every sparkling blue lake would catch the spirits that came up from behind—the ones smaller than a gnat, the others mean and large as a deer fly, and the few big as the giant bellowing moose. 'Then,' said Father Water with sad gentleness, 'I must lie down and die. Care for my body and know that my heart-place will be a shallow lake.' He disappeared, and the council fire died down and flickered out."

Plum Nelly stopped to bring Sandy another cup of hot, healing brew.

"The medicine men," continued Plum Nelly after Sandy drank, "looked upon a new land, a land dotted with lakes of bluest blue. They saw the spirits of the Land of Look-Behind drown in these lakes. And they saw something else, too—a mighty river ran through the forest where no river ever was before. They called the river Mississippi, meaning Father of Waters, in honor of Father Water. And they found the shallow lake that was the heart-place of Father Water and called this Lake Pepin and made it a place for mourning and for burying their dead. And Crossing Sky told me," Plum Nelly concluded, "that the Ohio River is one of Father Water's legs, and the Missouri River is the other leg."

Sandy thought a long time after Plum Nelly finished, sitting quietly in his chair and wrapped in a warm blanket. Then he said seriously, "Is that a true story, Plum Nelly?"

"I told it to you jest like Crossing Sky told it to me." Plum Nelly scratched the thinning brownish-red hair that somehow made his head look like an autumn weed patch. "I reckon it's true. Anyways, the Indians thought it was true. And there are lots of lakes, and the Mississippi is a

giant. Yup, and Lake Pepin for generations was the place where the Indians came to bury their dead and weep. It's true enough for me, Sandy."

Plum Nelly bustled off to his chores. And Sandy slept again, head lolling against the back of the chair. He slept peacefully, without dreaming, and the rest carried strength into his body. After a while, in the dim, faraway distance, he heard voices, but they were not strong enough to wake him.

The next thing he knew, a hand was on his shoulder and his father was saying, "How are you feeling now, Sandy?"

Sandy opened his eyes. Kit was on one side of him and his father on the other. Yellow Dog Dingo's cold nose nuzzled his hand. "Golly, Dad, you back? I feel better, lot's better. And—" Sandy thought a minute—"I'm starved!"

"You certainly look a lot better and your fever's gone. Those pills I gave you certainly fixed you up."

Sandy looked at Plum Nelly, and Plum Nelly looked at Sandy, but neither said anything. The brew of herbs was not mentioned. Plum Nelly just cleared his throat and hawed and hemmed a couple of times and said gruffly, "He's got to be all right if we're goin' to town tomorrow night."

"I didn't know we were going to town." Mr. Duncan swung around. "Plum Nelly, you didn't say a word to me about it."

"Shucks," said Plum Nelly, hastily hiding the brew kettle, "I always go ter town Saturday night. I git the package mail and look in on the dance. Have supper, too. Thought mebbe you'd like to go along. Don't have ter, if you don't want ter." He opened a can of beans. "It's sorta fun to put on war paint and drive in. Can't go dull as an old crow. Everybody dresses up fer Saturday night."

Kit looked up from unlacing high boots. "What's that about an old crow, Plum Nelly?"

"Why, don't you know?" Plum Nelly stopped right in the middle of emptying the bean can. "Well, what do yuh know?" He shook his head pityingly. "Don't you know why the crow is black, Kit?"

"Nope." Kit unlaced the other boot.

"It's like this," Plum Nelly began, adding salt pork and molasses to the beans: "In the beginning all birds were white. The robin didn't have his red breast, the wild canary wasn't splashed with yellow, the pheasant lacked his many-colored tail. One day the pheasant and the crow found a box of paints—blues and greens and scarlets and ground-browns and deep purples. Every color in the rainbow was in the box.

"So the pheasant and the crow decided to give the birds color. They sent out invitations and made appointments, like you do when you go to the dentist, Kit. One by one, the birds kept their appointments. From morning till night, the crow and the pheasant painted the birds, putting the blue on the bluebird, the orange on the oriole, the red on robin redbreast. Finally all was done. Only the pheasant and the crow were left. The crow worked hard coloring the pheasant. He was beautiful—really magnificent. Then the crow's turn came. The pheasant was in such a hurry to show off his new finery, he picked up the black paint and dumped it over the crow. That's why the crow is all black, and that's why he's got such a mean disposition—he never got over being disappointed."

"Did Crossing Sky tell you that, too?" Sandy walked to the stove and sniffed the aroma from the bean pot.

Plum Nelly set a pan of biscuits in the oven. "Crossing Sky didn't tell me everything I know. Go on now an' leave me to my victuals. Your pa and Kit are hungry. Tell 'em we'll eat jest as soon as I get it ready." He whistled a little tune and danced a little jig, kicking up his heels like a frisky colt in spring pasture.

The truth was, although he would not admit it, that Plum Nelly was having the time of his life with the Duncans. At times, especially in summer, the cabin was lonesome and even Broadwater Bay itself was lonely. So many people were around then—strangers, every one of them— that Plum Nelly felt ill at ease. Oh, he chatted and visited and set his tongue to small talk. And he smiled behind his hand at outlandish outfits vacationers put on, but he never got to know these in-and-outers who moved in, stayed two weeks, and moved out again. They couldn't be friendly neighbors. Plum Nelly enjoyed winter more than summer. No strangers churned the lake in speedboats then. He would rather be lonely than mix with outsiders. During winter's cold days and nights, when northern lights lit the sky with emeralds and rubies and twinkling diamonds, Plum Nelly sat snug in his cabin. The fireplace roared and the iron stove purred. He made cramped notes in his diary and brought his bird records up to date. He read and he stitched his flour-sack curtains. He repaired and painted casting plugs. His life was as peaceful as the snow-covered bay. Pulling a pan of hot biscuits from the oven, Plum Nelly thought again how glad he was to have his old friend

John Duncan with him. *Those boys are regular chips off the old block,* he said to himself.

After supper Plum Nelly brought out his fiddle, an ancient squeakbox that had seen better days. Holding it across a knee, Plum Nelly tightened the strings, then twanged them. Kit and Sandy were fascinated. They didn't believe the violin had a sweet note in it.

Plum Nelly guessed what the boys thought. "It's the apple of my eye," he said. He twanged again. "Oh, I guess fellers down in the city pay more fer fiddles—I gave all of sixteen dollars and two days' work cordin' wood for mine. But," Plum Nelly continued, "there ain't a fiddle I ever heard that's got a softer, truer tone than Old Molly here." His rough hands fondled the battered case. "I've heard tell that real good fiddles cost as much as fifty dollars. Never believed it, though. Mine's as good as any."

Mr. Duncan coughed, warning the boys not to interrupt and, above all, not to tell Plum Nelly that fifty dollars wouldn't buy a poor violin, let alone one of fine quality. Why, Kit's violin had cost more than a hundred dollars.

Plum Nelly tucked the fiddle under his chin and sawed the bow across the strings. The horrible screech sent Yellow Dog Dingo to his feet. He lifted his nose and howled. "Shucks—" Plum Nelly pointed the bow at Dingo—"I'm jest a-warmin' up, Dingo. Down, now! Don't go interruptin'." Dingo stood undecided, then trotted to a far corner and curled up, eyes suspicious.

Plum Nelly lifted the bow. Out from the fiddle drifted a melody sweet as clover honey and soft as pink clouds bumping together. He played "Barbry Allen," that song of sad love in the long ago. Then his foot went *tap-tap-tap* and the violin, spry and happy, burst into "Pop Goes the Weasel." Oh, Plum Nelly was really warmed up, sitting there in his favorite chair with his battered fiddle under his chin, his eyes half closed, and Kit and Sandy enjoying each note.

Every time Plum Nelly stopped, the boys clapped. "Go on, Plum Nelly, that's swell." And Plum Nelly did go on, playing songs that told of low bridge on the Erie Canal, of little dogies cavorting on the Far West plains, of Billy the Kid and that bad Denver Jim. The fiddle jogged, loped, cantered. It went *yippee-ti-yi* and laughed and hollered and cried with spirituals. It was no ordinary fiddle—the roundup was in it, and the storm at sea. The California gold miner, flirting with Lady Luck, was in it:

> *"Gold is got in pan and pot,*
> *Soup tureen and ladle,*
> *Basket, birdcage, and what not,*
> *Even to the cradle—*
> *Choose your able-bodied men,*
> *All whose arms are brawny,*
> *Give them picks and spades and then*
> *Off for Californy."*

Plum Nelly fiddled until sweat misted his brow and rained down his chin. And all the while his foot danced *tap-tap-tap*. Out of the fiddle came the frog that went a-courting and ole Jim Crow. Zip Coon and the Arkansas Traveler walked out big as life on the music and climbed Sourwood Mountain.

Then Plum Nelly broke off. "That's all," he said, wiping his brow. "That's all fer tonight."

"Just one more, Plum Nelly," Sandy pleaded.

"Please," Kit added.

Yellow Dog Dingo thumped an approving tail.

Plum Nelly mopped his brow, rubbing vigorously. "All right, just one more." He plucked a string. "This one tells a story—the tale of a traveler who came to Minnesota and found it the beauty of the West. Listen. I'll sing it and do better than a couple days ago."

Melody came from the fiddle, and Plum Nelly sang:

"Come all ye noble emigrants that are inclined to roam
Into this Western Country, to seek you out a home.
If you will be advised by me, I'll tell you what's the best,
Come settle in Minnesota, the Lily of the West.

"Now, this traveler," said Plum Nelly, "tried a lot of places first—Ohio and Illinois and even Michigan, but he didn't like any of them. Minnesota was the pleasant place for him.

"When I viewed this pleasant country, it filled me
with surprise,
To see those large prairies, and fields of grain
likewise;
You call into a cabin, you are always a welcome guest,
That's the fashion of Minnesota, the Lily of the West.

"I like the last stanza best of all." The fiddle sang again:

"The Gopher Girls are cunning, the Gopher girls are shy;
I'll marry me a Gopher Girl, or a bachelor I'll die,
I'll wear a standing collar, support a handsome wife,
And live in Minnesota the balance of my life!"

"How about one more, Plum Nelly?" Mr. Duncan grinned broadly. "That's a great song."

Plum Nelly cased his precious violin. "Nope—that's all fer tonight. Hike to bed, fellers. Sandy needs a lot of rest to kill the rest of his cold. Kit, you better turn in, too, if we're goin' ter the dance tomorrow."

11 Swing Your Partners!

Saturday night in the north country is Christmas, Fourth of July, and circus day rolled into one jolly evening. It's a rip-roaring holiday and comes once a week. The Saturday dance is always the same—and always different. Everybody who isn't sick-a-bed finishes chores early, puts on better than Sunday best, and skylarks for town and fun.

Plum Nelly started primping before day, as soon as first light touched the lake, turning it from ink black to dark blue. He scurried around the cabin like a chicken with its head cut off. He hurried Kit and Sandy through their bacon and sunny-side-up eggs, and rushed Mr. Duncan through his coffee. Mr. Duncan liked to dawdle over morning coffee. Plum Nelly scolded a blue jay that came for crumbs, and the saucy jay scolded right back. Plum Nelly even forgot to give Yellow Dog Dingo an after-breakfast biscuit. And Dingo begged hard, sitting up pert-like with pink tongue drooling.

"First off," Plum Nelly said to nobody in particular, "I've got ter press my shirt. Only wear it on special occasions. Should've done it yesterday." He spread an orange and lavender sport shirt on the table. The old-fashioned flatiron weighed about eight pounds. A drawer in the iron's bottom held hot coals. Plum Nelly filled the iron's firebox, dribbling sparks.

"You'll set the place on fire," warned Mr. Duncan.

"Got this here iron thirty years ago . . ." Plum Nelly glared, busy pressing, ". . . at a country sale. Best iron there is. Never burned the place down yet."

Finally the shirt was finished, although Kit noticed wrinkles around the neck. Plum Nelly hung it over the back of a chair.

"What time we going, Plum Nelly?" Kit asked.

"Soon as I git ready. Them that ask foolish questions get foolish answers!"

"You mean this morning?"

"Great guns and pickled pigs' feet! It's going to rush me like thunder to get away by four o'clock." Plum Nelly looked at his watch. "Don't know if I can make it then. But I never git there later than five." He banged out, headed for the barn.

All day Plum Nelly fluttered, until the boys, too, caught the fidgets. He wasted more time worrying over what he had to do than if he'd done it. First off, he polished his boots with lampblack. Then he remembered the jeep needed washing. He brushed half his hat and ran down to the minnow house to find his gloves. He was crazy as a black kitten in a field of green catnip. He shaved and slapped bay rum on his leathery cheeks. The bay rum stung, and Plum Nelly whooped and yelled as though he were being murdered. He couldn't recall where he'd left his necktie. He laid out his clothes, and a few minutes later carefully hung them up again. At lunch he poured salt in his coffee and sugared the soup.

Yet with all his fussing and squirrel-jumping, Plum Nelly wasn't ready when four o'clock rolled around. He'd broken a boot lace. Kit and Sandy were in their go-to-meeting best. Their father, who didn't like to dress up, put on a clean khaki shirt and a brand new hunting coat that wasn't grease-spotted. Still Plum Nelly stayed in his room.

Finally his door flew open. Plum Nelly was prouder than a peacock and twice as colorful.

Kit took one look and closed his eyes. "Jeepers!"

Sandy said, "Oh bro-*ther!*" Then he said it again. "Oh bro-*ther!*"

Mr. Duncan coughed as though something had stuck in his throat all of a sudden.

No doubt about it, Plum Nelly was a sight. His pants were plaid—red and black in big squares about the size of a checkerboard. His shirt was the favorite orange and lavender. A purple tie was knotted around his neck, and right in the tie's center was a brass horseshoe stickpin. But that wasn't all. A yellow pork-pie hat sat jauntily atop his reddish-brown hair.

"What yuh lookin' at?" Plum Nelly scowled. "Come on —we're late already." He paraded to the jeep.

Longville's main street was packed with cars. There were battered trucks and station wagons with duckboats on top. Sandy pointed out a jeep as ancient as Plum Nelly's. Shoppers jostled one another and pushed in and out of the general store. On the corner, the constable, star gleaming on red suspender, talked with a game warden in natty uniform and broad-brimmed hat of forest green.

"We'll jest sit in the car a spell,"—Plum Nelly eased the jeep into a parking space—"an' watch the folks. It pleasures me to jest sit and see folks." He kindled his pipe. Now that he was in town, he seemed in no hurry.

Mr. Duncan left to buy a new fishline. Plum Nelly was content to lounge in the jeep, watch the people, and hail friends. But the boys soon tired of doing nothing. Kit noticed that most of the crowd was heading for the firehouse.

"What's everybody going to the fire station for?" Kit nudged Plum Nelly to get his attention.

Plum Nelly looked down the street. "Guess we better be goin' there, too." He slid from under the wheel. "Come on, fellers."

"Why?" said Sandy, climbing out. Kit followed.

But Plum Nelly was already striding along without waiting for the boys. He bowed right and left to friends and stopped to shake hands. Sandy ran to keep up. "What's so important at the firehouse?" he wanted to know.

"The church ladies are laying out a bean supper." Plum

Nelly grabbed Sandy's elbow to hurry him along. "Best thing is to get there early and pick out a cake."

"Pick out a cake?" Kit and Sandy were puzzled.

"Sure," grinned Plum Nelly, weaving through the crowd. "It's this way—pigs is pigs, but cakes are something mighty special." He waved to his old friends Peg and Andy Kennedy, resort owners on Girl Lake. "Yup," Plum Nelly went on, "cakes are different. There are white cakes with chocolate icing, chocolate cakes with white frosting, layer cakes with maple icing, and maple cakes with strawberry frosting." He drew a deep breath. "Then there's layer cakes—one, two, three layers. Some are all the same flavor, and others are different. Maybe one layer's chocolate, the next orange, the next pineapple. You'll see when we get there. There's always angel foods, sunshines, and spice cakes. Most cakes are purty good, but some wimmen can't bake a cake for sour apples. That's why we're goin' now. See?"

"No," Sandy said, but his mouth watered just the same. Plum Nelly bent down to Sandy's ear. "Can't say more now," he whispered. "Jest follow me up the stairs. You'll learn what I mean."

They took their place in a line that moved slowly through the brick firehouse. The line curved past the old ladder truck and around a spanking new pumper. It crept up the stairway to Longville's recreation hall. There Plum Nelly bought tickets. Each ticket read: GOOD FOR ONE DINNER AND DANCE.

Paper streamers festooned the hall's rafters and decorated a raised platform on which stood an upright piano. The Stars and Stripes hung from one wall, and on another was a big picture of Teddy Roosevelt in a Rough Rider's uniform. But the tables caught the boys' eyes—long tables running the length of the room; tables set with knives, forks, spoons, and crockery dishes. Around each table people pushed and shoved.

"See what I mean now?" Plum Nelly pointed.

Down the center of each table stood a row of cakes. Between the cakes were dishes of dill pickles. Kit and Sandy had never seen so many different kinds of cake at one party. Plum Nelly was right: there were chocolate cakes with vanilla icing, and white cakes with chocolate frosting, and cakes topped with whipped cream and strawberries. Layer cakes, angel foods, pound cakes, a lemon-jelly cake. There was a cake baked in the form of a lamb and covered with woolly coconut. The lamb wore a blue ribbon around its neck.

"Now," said Plum Nelly, "see what I mean?"

Sandy shook his head. All he could see was more cakes than he ever knew existed.

"Come here!" Plum Nelly yanked Sandy into a corner. "Listen, you! What do you suppose all these people are walkin' round the tables for?"

"I dunno."

"Then I'll tell you. They're pickin' out the cake they want for dessert. They know the good ones from the bad. They know Mrs. Swenson's been bakin' fer a lifetime and still turns out frosted rocks—nobody can eat her cakes." He snorted. "But Old Lady Johnson's angel foods," Plum Nelly went on enthusiastically, "they'll melt in a man's mouth. Light as a feather and tender as a moonbeam they be. I'm the best cake judge in these parts—maybe in the whole danged world. Jest follow me and grab a seat quick when I tell yuh."

Spry as a billy goat, Plum Nelly marched around the pastry-laden tables. He squinted at the round cakes with pink icings and examined square cakes decorated with clusters of sugar flowers and peered like a judge at tiered layer cakes. And all this time he made little cheerful chirpings. Sandy kept close to Plum Nelly. All the cakes looked tasty and beautiful to him.

"Here we be!" Plum Nelly stopped suddenly. Right in front was a three-layer sponge cake topped with an ocean of whipped cream and dotted with red cherries. "That's Dorothy Dailey's cake. It's got custard between the layers."

Mr. Duncan had joined them during their tour of inspection, and now he sat down beside Kit. A tall farmer in clean bibbed overalls sat next to Sandy at the other side of the table. "Name's Thompson," he said, putting out a rough hand. "Derby Thompson. I've known Plum Nelly a good many years and I've learned to sit close to him at these shindigs. The rascal really knows cake."

The beans came in—big ones and little ones. Saturday-night suppers always start with beans. Up in the north country folks are divided into mighty strong camps on the question of peace beans and war beans. Some won't touch large peace beans, and others turn up noses at the small war beans, even though both kinds are baked exactly alike. Plum Nelly was a peace-bean man, so Sandy took big beans. Across the table, Kit and his father piled their plates with the smaller war beans. Sandy noticed that Uncle Bert at the next table had a plate of peace beans.

"Mr. Thompson," Sandy said, turning to the farmer in

overalls, "what kind of a bean man are you—peace or war?"

The farmer laughed. "Oh, I'm a peace-beaner like Plum Nelly." He passed pickles and brown bread to Sandy. "You see," Mr. Thompson continued, "when Plum Nelly and I settled up here, we could get only large beans. But those big New England beans didn't grow right in our cold weather. I planted half a bushel the first year and not a one growed.

"Next season I planted horse-radish next to my beans. Horse-radish was just hot enough to warm the plants and help them grow. Got a fine crop, too, only they were smaller and a mite hotter than big beans. That's the difference between peace beans and war beans—the one's bigger and milder, the other's smaller and hotter. That's what folks say, anyhow. And that's why both kinds come to table at these suppers." Mr. Thompson filled his plate again. "War beans have more get-up-and-go to them, but peace beans, like old friends, comfort a man more."

"I see," said Sandy, but he thought the whole idea silly. "And—"

Plum Nelly interrupted. "Cake-cuttin' time!"

He sliced the luscious sponge cake, cutting generous slices. Each piece was bountifully smothered in whipped cream and cherries. Up and down the other tables people were "oh-ing" over their cakes. To Sandy, Mrs. Dailey's cake was everything Plum Nelly had promised. It was fluffy light, the way a sponge cake should be. The custard filling was smooth, the way custard should be when it isn't filled with truck like cornstarch. And the whipped cream was yellow thick, the way real country cream is. Sandy ate three pieces. It was worth coming to town for a dinner like this.

After dessert, Uncle Bert led volunteers in taking down the tables and stacking chairs in a corner of the hall. Up on the raised platform three fiddlers rosined bows. A youngish piano player tickled off a scale or two.

"Is that all the orchestra?" asked Kit, coming up to Plum Nelly.

"Sure, and why not?"

"Well," said Kit, "it looks mighty small. We've got a bigger orchestra in school."

"Great guns and pickled pigs' feet! What good's a big band? Jest makes a lot of noise, that's all. These fellers beat any city orchestra yuh ever saw. You wait and see."

The boys didn't wait long. Up on the platform stepped Carl the Caller. He held up a hand for quiet. "La-dies and gen-tlemen!" His voice was like a thunderstorm. "La-dies and gen-tlemen! I'm going to call the tunes an' you're going to dance to 'em. Don't be shy. Not that you ever are." He hitched up his pants and snapped his red suspenders. "Get set! Take your partners and circle round!"

With a *whoop-dee-do*, the crowd formed a circle. In the mad rush for the floor the Duncans were pushed to the wall, but Plum Nelly, pork-pie hat bobbing, elbowed into the ring.

"Let 'er go!" shouted Carl the Caller. The piano and fiddles broke into:

> *"Flies in the buttermilk, two by two,*
> *Flies in the buttermilk, shoo fly shoo,*
> *Flies in the buttermilk, two by two,*
> *Skip to my Lou, my darlin'."*

Into the ring stepped a girl in gingham and a boy in high boots and hunting clothes. Quick as a wink they formed an arch with their arms. Other dancers ducked beneath. All of a sudden there was Plum Nelly, doffing his yellow hat in grand manner and singing at the top of his lungs:

> *"Chicken in the bread pan, scratchin' out dough,*
> *Chicken in the bread pan, scratchin' out dough,*
> *Chicken in the bread pan, scratchin' out dough,*
> *Skip to my Lou, my darlin'."*

How the dancers clapped and cheered. The fiddlers hit high notes, laughing notes, that called "Skip to my Lou." Uncle Bert, Yankee eyes twinkling, took the next verse, shoving Plum Nelly aside.

> *"Caint git a fat gal, skinny gal'll do,*
> *Caint git a fat gal, skinny gal'll do,*
> *Caint git a fat gal, skinny gal'll do,*
> *Skip to my Lou, my darlin'."*

"Folks," yelled Carl the Caller when the applause died, "that's only the beginning. The evening's young an' so are you. Come on, now, the first is just the beginning. Plum Nelly and Bert showed the way. You take if from there." He turned to the skinny piano player. "Hit 'er up, Eddie my boy!"

Eddie, head thrown back, raised hands above the keyboard. Down they swooped in a smashing chord. The violins joined, the caller clapped out the time, the dancers whooped and hollered.

With Eddie's first tingling notes, the Duncans were

swept from the wall into a queue of merry dancers. Kit was flung from hand to hand. Sandy found himself bowing to a fat lady who, for all her two hundred pounds, was light of foot. She whirled Sandy around faster than a hungry trout gobbles a fly. And Mr. Duncan, dignity forgotten, did a stately turn-around with a bearded trapper.

Ladies moved out and gents moved in. Carl, the wild-voiced caller, hurried the speed. This was Saturday night in the north country, and time was not to be wasted.

> *"First couple out and swing in the middle.*
> *Shake your big feet to the tune of the fiddle.*
> *When you get there remember my call.*
> *Swing on the corner and promenade all."*

Excitement crept into Kit's bones and bubbled his blood. His feet patterned the quick steps and the slow steps and the mincing half steps by themselves. Kit didn't have to tell his feet what to do—they just naturally followed Eddie's piano and the violins for the time of their life. Kit puffed and panted. After beans and brown bread and three helpings of cake, his breath struggled out and sweat ran down his face. He jerked his necktie and opened his collar.

> *"I'm Captain Jinks of the Horse Marines,*
> *I feed my horse on corn and beans."*

"Golly," Kit said to Sandy after a quadrille, "I'm pooped."

"Me too!" Sandy's face was beet red.

"Plum Nelly's fresh as a daisy," Kit said.

"He's used to it—here we go again."

Carl the Caller spieled, "La-dies and escorts!" He waved down applause. "La-dies and gen-tlemen! That was fine, but not good enough. We're whoopin' it up tonight. Forget your worries and forget taxes! Let's have more vinegar, more ginger, more you-know-what!" The crowd cheered. "That's better! There's goin' to be a hot time in the old town tonight! Swing your ma, swing your pa, and don't forget Old Arkansaw!"

The boys learned to turkey-wing, jigged to the lilting tune of "Irish Washerwoman," did an old-time polka, and had a lesson in the barn-dance schottische. Sandy danced so hard in the polka that he stumbled and fell smack on his face. And Kit was puffing and red of face when intermission came.

"Land o' Goshen," Plum Nelly gasped, "let's set a spell." He led the way to a corner bench. A few minutes later Mr. Duncan came pushing through the crowd and joined them.

"Here come the church ladies with refreshments," he told Plum Nelly.

" 'Bout time," said Plum Nelly. "Dancin' sure whets my appetite. Can't remember when I ate last."

"If you want to know, you ate just an hour and a half ago," Sandy piped up.

"That long?" yelped Plum Nelly. "No wonder I'm wolfish."

He helped himself from a huge tray of warm sugar-sprinkled doughnuts. Mr. Duncan fetched mugs of coffee and milk.

"That's better," said Plum Nelly when Mr. Duncan came weaving back through the celebrators with a cup in each hand. He walked carefully so as not to spill the coffee.

"You boys gettin' enough sinkers?" Plum Nelly looked anxiously at their plates. "Yup, guess you are." He chewed peacefully. "Nothin' much better," he went on, "than fried, crunchy-like doughnuts. They're sweet to the taste and consolin' to the stomach."

"I sure like 'em," said Sandy, stuffing his mouth full.

"Doughnuts," said Plum Nelly pridefully, "were invented right up here. I saw it happen."

"Now, Plum Nelly," warned Kit, who suspected Plum Nelly was going to tell another whopper.

"True as gospel." Plum Nelly was so serious the boys believed him. "Yup, I was on the spot when Hog Jowl Swanson invented doughnuts. 'Bout the biggest thing ever happened in the north country, exceptin', of course, fishin' an' huntin' and maybe Paul Bunyan."

"You sure you aren't spoofing us?" Kit had never thought about who invented doughnuts, and he was still a little suspicious. One second he thought Plum Nelly was telling the truth; the next, he was not so sure.

Plum Nelly looked hurt by Kit's doubts. "Here's what happened," he said. "Judge fer yourself. This whole country once was timberland, every last inch of it. When loggin' was goin' great shakes and guns, a little shrimp of a man, bow-legged and tight-fisted, opened a hotel. More of a boardinghouse, it was. Hog Jowl's fame as a cook spread far and wide. Lumberjacks came miles for his venison steaks and roast of black bear an' planked bass.

"I boarded for a spell with Hog Jowl up on the Big Fork. I still recollect his victuals—big plum puddings steamed in a washtub, giant griddlecakes flopped with a pitchfork, they wuz so big, mountains of mashed potatoes beat light with a canoe paddle. Oh, Hog Jowl could cook, all right. He was a regular whiz at everything but baking. His bread was concrete, his pies tougher'n an elk's hoof, his biscuits wuz boulders. We hid Hog Jowl's pastry under our shirts and dumped it in the woods. The jacks never wanted to hurt Hog Jowl's feelings none, 'cause, other than pastry, he cooked better than any spoon-stirrin' female.

"Trouble was, Hog Jowl was plumb crazy 'bout hot breads and cakes—the only things he couldn't cook, he kept makin'. Many a night I've seen him a-sittin' by the stove, readin' recipes and mutterin' an' groanin' to himself. Next day he'd try a new cake. But they'd come out of the oven with high sides and low middles like a buckboard. You couldn't eat 'em. I used to drill the centers out and use 'em to run rope through. Some jacks punched holes in 'em and soldered 'em to their rifles for peep sights.

"One day I jest couldn't stand it no longer and up and told Hog Jowl his cakes weren't fit fer man or beast. He was just slippin' a pan into the oven. Well, the poor feller turned pink and then red and back to pink agin, he wuz so mad. 'Some fallers tenk dey yump on me, eh? Ay s'pose yu tenk ay don't run gude place!' he yelled. With that he heaved the cakes into a pot of grease bubblin' on the range and shot out of the kitchen like a long-tailed, double-bitted, fire-eatin' hudag was on his trail an'—"

"Golly," said Sandy, "where did he go?"

"Don't rightly remember." Plum Nelly drained his coffee. "But I know Hog Jowl was gone four nights and three days. I—because of my big mouth—did all the cookin'. That's how doughnuts were invented."

Kit was puzzled. "What do you mean?"

"I was fixin' to throw out the cakes frying in the hot grease, when I jest thought I'd taste one. They looked kinda good, bubblin' and sizzlin' in the kettle. And great guns and pickled pigs' feet, they wuz so lickin' tasty, I served 'em for supper. The jacks let out a whoop and carried me round on their shoulders shouting, 'Plum Nelly's made the best cakes ever cooked!' They swore they never wanted Hog Jowl back.

"Then I got feelin' sorry fer Hog Jowl, remembering his rare venison steaks, his plum puddings steamed in the washtub, his roast of black bear smothered in wild onions, his mashed potatoes beat with a birch paddle. 'Hold up!' I yells to the lumberjacks, eatin' the world's first doughnuts by the handful. 'Hold up! I didn't make them doodads. Hog Jowl did—he left 'em fer a surprise.'

"I jest couldn't bear to take the credit. I remembered how hard Hog Jowl tried and how mad and sad he wuz when I said his cakes weren't fit fer fowl or flesh. So I gave Hog Jowl all the credit. To this day, nobody except you boys knows that I, Plum Nelly Jones, really invented the doughnut. And," he concluded slyly, "I don't want you to breathe it to a soul."

"I won't," Sandy said solemnly.

After a time Kit said, "Well, I won't either, if you don't want me to, but it still sounds a little peculiar to me."

Plum Nelly waggled his head sorrowfully. "Never mind," he said, "it's dance time again."

Kit and Sandy hitched up their belts and pushed to the center of the floor. Carl, the leather-lunged caller, shouted for a Virginia reel. The violins capered, and Eddie did tricks with the piano keys.

> *"Head lady and foot gent forward and back.*
> *Forward and swing with the right hand 'round."*

Up the center and down the outside went Kit and Sandy. They formed an arch and balanced through. They forwarded with left hand 'round and both hands 'round. They followed the fiddles' *do-si-do* until the last dance was over and the crowd sang "Good night ladies, we're goin' to leave you now."

Plum Nelly was carrying a cardboard box when he climbed into the jeep. "Don't go squashin' that," he said on the drive home.

"What's in it?" Sandy's legs ached and he was sleepy, but he wasn't too tired to ask questions.

"Well, you see, I kinda thought I might be a mite hungry when I got home." Plum Nelly whipped into the Woodtick Trail. "So I jest bought an extry cake—chocolate —an' four dozen doughnuts."

12 *Sandy's Big Adventure*

"Did I ever tell yuh," asked Plum Nelly, " 'bout the time I ate a big old he-bear with his own teeth?"

Plum Nelly lazed on the dock, doing nothing in particular but squinting with kindly eyes across the bay and watching a breeze riffle a stand of wild rice. The boys were hunkered down beside him. Sandy picked a backlash out of his casting line, working carefully with a little pointed stick and grumbling at the snarl of twisted knots. Kit lay on his back counting cloud patches as they raced by.

"Eat a bear with his own teeth!" Kit sat up quick-like. "What do you mean, Plum Nelly?"

"Oh, 'twarn't much." Plum Nelly tilted his hat for shade. "You see, it was this way. I was berry pickin' out there on Pew's Point, carrying a tin pail and no gun. Bears weren't in my mind. I got ter pickin', movin' from one bush to another, thinkin' what a good pie the berries would make and payin' no 'tention much to where I wuz goin'. All of a sudden I looks up and there, right in front of me, standin' on his hind legs and reachin' fer my pail of berries with a paw as big as an Easter ham, wuz a black bear. A big old he-bear. I kin see him right now—fur scratchy enough to make a suit for the devil, and leetle red eyes that blazed like a forest fire."

"Golly," said Sandy, dropping his fishline.

"That old he-bear," Plum Nelly went on, "wasn't goin' to steal my blueberries, no sir! I ups and bangs him over the head with my pail, knockin' the wits out of him. Then I lets the air out of him with my hunting knife. I got scratched up some, you bet, an' my coat wuz torn to ribbons. I wuz mad. So mad I knocked old Mr. Bear's teeth right out. When I got back to the cabin I fixed up a set of false teeth for me to wear when eatin' tough meat. And I ate that old he-bear with his own teeth. I'll show you his skin one of these days."

"That's just too much, Plum Nelly," Sandy said indignantly. "I'm going for a walk." And he stalked off.

"Don't git into trouble," Plum Nelly called. "Storm clouds are brewing."

Sandy pretended not to hear.

The boy wandered past the ice house and barn to a trail

that struck off into the woods. He had never noticed this path before. He followed it carelessly, not looking whether it went north or south or east or west. Sandy was too busy muttering "bear-with-its-own-teeth, bear-with-its-own-teeth" to pay any attention to direction. Soon the lonely pines and dark evergreens closed behind him and the trail disappeared. When Sandy turned to look for it, it wasn't there. It was as if all of a sudden a magic broom had swept a thick carpet of pine needles over the path.

A lively chipmunk ran through the woods. Sandy followed him, but the bright-eyed little fellow with waving tail didn't seem to be going anywhere. He'd run up a tree and down again, his striped tail fluttering and his voice making the chirping talk that chipmunks do when excited. Then he disappeared as quietly and mysteriously as the path had done. And Sandy was left alone.

He knew now that he was lost.

When Sandy felt for his new compass he remembered he'd left it on his bunk. When he looked for the sun, it was covered with purple-black clouds. A wind came sweeping from the sudden storm clouds, shivering the tall pine tops and tossing the evergreens. Far-off thunder rumbled. Sandy turned and ran, dodging windfalls, stumbling over moss-green logs, ducking through underbrush that closed tighter with every step.

A fork of lightning snapped at him, and the sky spilled buckets of rain. It soaked Sandy's windbreaker in a jiffy and sopped his jeans. His legs were wet up to his knees. He ran and ran until he thought he could run no more.

Just then he broke out of the timber and came face to face with a hill. In its side was the yawning mouth of a cave. Sandy popped in faster than you can say "rabbit-in, rabbit-out." But even before he shook his wet shoulders and looked around, he knew there was something special about this cave. He could *feel* it. There was a tingling in his bones that said "Be careful!"

At first Sandy was afraid, fearful of the dim light, of the dank coolness that seeped from rock walls, of rotting rafters hewn years ago with a lumberjack's ax. He thought of the big he-bear that Plum Nelly had eaten with its own ugly teeth and wondered if this were a bear's den. He wished now that he hadn't left Plum Nelly and his brother on the dock, and he wondered if they missed him.

Sandy turned and peered hard into the cavern, squinting to see better, but all he saw was a dismal tunnel of darkness that stretched back and back into the hill. He shivered and stayed close to the entrance, watching pelting rain that flattened windfalls, and listening to thunder drum in the sky.

"I'm sure a boob," he said aloud, "getting lost this way."

Behind him a deep voice boomed: "I'm sure a boob, getting lost this way."

Sandy jumped. Then he laughed and called, "Boo-o-o-oo."

And the echo answered, "Boo-o-o-oo!"

The echo was so friendly, now that Sandy knew what it was, that he kept up a steady conversation while he wrung out his sodden clothes—first the jacket, then the pants. It was good to have somebody to talk to, even if it was only an echo. He turned the water out of his shoes. Away down in his shirt pocket he found a match. He remembered he had put it there one morning when helping Plum Nelly burn a brush pile. Very carefully, Sandy scratched together dry twigs from the cave floor and dragged up a few chunks of wood. He worked as if building this fire was the most important job he'd ever done. A handful of brittle leaves went under the twigs. The match flared and wavered, then the leaves caught. In a minute the sticks blazed. Sandy added wood to the fire.

The first tiny flame turned the cave from a dismal hideout into a comfortable retreat. Sandy felt better right away. And when the chunks crackled and sputtered, sending out light and heat, the comfortable retreat became mighty homelike. The fire dried Sandy's clothes and sent dancing fingers of light down the black tunnel.

"I wonder what's back there?"

"I wonder what's back there?" said the echo.

"Can't you do anything but repeat?" Sandy asked crossly. "Why don't you try answering for a change?" But the echo wouldn't answer.

Sandy fashioned a torch from dry branches, made sure his fire would keep, and, one slow foot at a time, started down the tunnel, holding the torch high. One foot after another, and always looking to see where the next step should be. On and on, turning when the tunnel turned, stepping cautiously lest he tumble into a pit. One slow foot after another until, a little ahead, he saw a ribbon of daylight push through the darkness. A dozen more steps, and he walked into an underground room with rock walls and a high ceiling. Daylight came from a hole in the ceiling.

This dry, warm place with a scattering of leaves on the floor wasn't a bear's snug den for the long winter sleep, nor was it the neat home of a fox with sharp-nosed children. Enough light seeped through the roof for Sandy to make out bunks and chairs and a strong table of notched logs. Smart as bears and foxes are, they aren't bright enough to hammer together furniture. The thought of a clumsy bear doing carpentry made Sandy grin.

He looked around again. A stone fireplace filled one wall. A huge, burned-out tree stump lay nearby. Sandy didn't like the looks of it. Close to it was a pile of wood, each piece the same length. There was even a crane set into the fireplace. And on the crane hung a tarnished brass kettle.

"Somebody lives here!" Sandy gasped.

Then he spied age-old cobwebs thick on the bunks, deep dust on the massive table, heaps of lifeless ashes in the fireplace. The air smelled stale and dead. Sandy realized no human being had come here for a long, long time.

To keep new prickles of fear away, Sandy talked out loud. Not even the friendly echo kept him company now.

"I'm lost, and I'm in a deserted cave, and it's raining cats and dogs." Sandy felt sorry for himself.

He went on talking while his eyes roamed over the strange room he'd discovered. "Plum Nelly says to keep cool when you're lost—but I'm going to keep warm! Yes, sir, I'm going to build a fire and stay right here till the storm is over."

Shoving away gray ashes with a thin slab took a long time, but finally the fireplace was clean. Sandy made a tepee of leaves and twigs. He lit the tinder with his torch, and when it caught and the draft pulled smoke up the flue, he put heavier wood on the blaze. Soon the room was as

toasty as Plum Nelly's kitchen. The boy wished he wasn't alone. He wished he could hear Plum Nelly's "great guns and pickled pigs' feet," and his father telling him it was time to do the dishes. Sandy thought of Kit, and wondered what Yellow Dog Dingo was doing.

On his next trip from the woodpile, Sandy stopped in amazement. He looked again to make sure he'd seen right. Sure enough, in a dark corner leaned a rifle, an old-fashioned gun with long barrel and powder pan. Sandy dropped the wood, the pieces spilling from his arms with a clatter. He moved slowly to the rifle, reaching out to touch it and quickly drawing back. What if it were loaded? Plum Nelly always said never to touch a gun if it was loaded. Sandy got a stick and poked gingerly at the rifle. He saw dark rust on it. He put down the stick and picked up the rifle carefully. It was so heavy the barrel wavered when he lifted it to his shoulder. He put it down, panting.

"Now, how do you suppose it got here?" he said.

He caught up the gun and carried it to the fire. Sitting tailor-fashion on the floor, Sandy rubbed it with his handkerchief. The stock was smooth, as if the sweat of many hands had polished it. There was a metal plate on the rifle. And when Sandy wiped the grime from it, he saw clear as anything the picture of a stag running through the woods. It was time for more firewood, and Sandy laid the gun down carefully.

When he hurried back to the fire, he had a piece of wood in one hand and a curious metal flask in the other: a stoppered brass bottle green with mold. Sandy pitched the log on the fire and began cleaning the flask. He rubbed off the filth, getting his handkerchief so dirty that he threw it away and used his shirttail.

"What do you think of that?" he muttered to himself. "It's the powder flask that belongs with the rifle. Oh bro-*ther!* Is this something!"

The powder horn had more pictures on it than did the old rifle. There was a hunter carrying a long rifle and a bear raring up on hind legs. There was a boy in coonskin cap and a skulking wolf. There was a fierce-looking Indian lurking behind a tree with tomahawk upraised. That much was plain, but there was plenty more beneath the dirt that Sandy couldn't make out, no matter how hard he rubbed.

Sandy sat for a long time with the wonderful rifle across his knees and the brass powder flask in his lap. The fire's heat reached out to lull him and make his eyes heavy. When he awoke, the fire was almost out and he heard no rain or thunder drumming across the sky. "I'd best be getting home," he said.

Scrambling up, he hefted the heavy rifle and put the grimy powder flask into a jacket pocket. Down the tunnel he went and out to the entrance of the cave. Making sure that the fire there was out, Sandy stepped into sunlight so bright it hurt his eyes. He blinked in the brightness that so often comes after a sudden storm in the north country.

"Now then"—Sandy looked all around—"which way is home?" He puffed up the steep hill that sheltered the strange cave. From the top he looked down a long valley and out over a lake with a broad bay. There, right before his eyes and looking for all the world like a miniature camp, was Plum Nelly's cabin and barn and icehouse. "Why, I must have walked in a circle in the storm."

Grasping the rifle firmly, Sandy set out, being careful to keep his bearings and not lose himself again. It never would do to get lost twice on the same day. The old gun was heavy, so ponderous that Sandy wondered how pioneers ever moved quickly with such weapons. Every time he picked up the rifle after resting, it was heavier than when he had set it down. But he stumbled on, now running a little and now pausing to suck in breath.

The middle of the afternoon was almost gone when Sandy and long rifle and powder flask plodded wearily across Plum Nelly's yard. His feet hurt, and his jacket was torn by creepers. Yet he marched jauntily up the steps and walked into the kitchen stiff with pride.

Plum Nelly, sorting fall potatoes, glanced up, looked again, and scrambled to his feet, spilling dirty spuds on a clean floor. "Sandy! Great guns and pickled pigs' feet, where you been, lad?" Plum Nelly looked again. "An' where in tarnation did you get that blunderbuss? Here, let me see it. You're all dirty an' yer coat looks like you was clawed by a wildcat!" Plum Nelly let out a bellow. "John! Sandy's home an' so taggered I wouldn't set him in a field for a scarecrow."

Mr. Duncan and Kit came running. "Where you been, boy?"

"Yeh," Kit said, "we were just about to go looking for you."

Sandy looked his brother straight in the eye. "I been lost," he said defiantly.

He set the rifle down. "An' I found a cave and a tunnel

and an underground room with furniture and a fireplace. And this gun and a powder horn, too." He glared at Kit. "I guess you never found anything like that! What's more," he added, "I found my way home, too."

Kit grabbed for the rifle. "Where did you find the gun?"

"And the powder horn?" asked Mr. Duncan.

Plum Nelly said nothing; he even pretended that Sandy's coming home with a powder horn and ancient rifle was nothing out of the ordinary. He set about picking up the spilled potatoes.

"I found 'em in a cave." Sandy smoothed the rifle with a hand trembling with pride. He looked at Plum Nelly, but still Plum Nelly didn't say a word. "Well," Sandy said impatiently, "why don't you say something?"

Deliberately Plum Nelly scooped the last spud into a pan and reached for a paring knife. "Don't know there's much to say," he said mildly. Then he added, "Let's see the gun."

Sandy handed it to him, and Plum Nelly looked for a long, silent time. Finally he said, "You found this in a cave? Where?"

Sandy told how he'd lost his way in the sudden storm, and how he just happened to see the cave's mouth when he came out of the woods. "I was just lost, Plum Nelly, and I'd lost my bearings. It served me right, I suppose, for leaving my compass home." He described the passage that led to the room of furniture. He told about the burned-out, evil-looking stump that lay by the fireplace full of long-dead ashes.

Plum Nelly nodded, and Sandy thought he wasn't going to say a word. Finally the guide puffed out his cheeks and blew a question at the boy. "Are you tellin' the truth, lad?"

"Honor bright," Sandy said quickly.

"Great guns and pickled pigs' feet! That must be it, then. Yup, that must be it!"

"Must be what?" asked Mr. Duncan, who was as bewildered as Sandy at Plum Nelly's behavior.

"Well, now, I'll tell you, but maybe you won't believe it." Plum Nelly picked up the paring knife and ran a thumb along its keen edge. "Sandy here stumbled across the hiding place of a gang that robbed the town bank 'way back when. They never was—"

"A real robbers' cave!" Kit jumped up and down. Yellow Dog Dingo snuffled the rifle, and the fur on his back went up.

"Can't you ever be quiet?" Plum Nelly sounded out-of-sorts, but his eyes twinkled. "It was this way," he went on after a minute. "The cave that Sandy found was first used by lumberjacks a long time ago when this country was first cut over. Stories say that explorers used it before the jacks did. I don't know fer certain about that. Anyway, it was warm and snug and dry, better than any cabin even in the dead of winter. The jacks fixed it up real nice. Then all the timber hereabouts was cut, and the loggers moved on. The cave was forgotten.

"Years later the town bank wuz robbed, as I told you, an' the thieves got away without ever bein' caught. It's always been said they holed up fer a spell in the cave, but nobody ever proved it, especially with the haunted stump there—"

"Haunted stump? What do you mean?" Sandy was puzzled.

Plum Nelly didn't answer. Picking up the rifle, he squinted down the long barrel.

"Say, Plum Nelly," said Sandy, reaching for the gun, "can I keep this—and the powder flask, too? Can I take them home with me and show them at school? Can I, Plum Nelly? Please!"

"Don't see why not." Plum Nelly turned the flask in his hands. "They don't belong to anybody now. I don't rightly know who owned 'em first—'pears to me like they belonged to some explorer that came this way long before the loggers." He passed the flask to Kit. "Why don't you and Kit keep 'em together—sort of a partnership, you know."

But Kit, to everybody's surprise, handed the brass flask right back to Sandy. "You keep it," he said firmly. "You found it and it's yours. I want the stump."

Plum Nelly roared. "You want what?"

Kit's face grew red, but he stood up bravely to Plum Nelly, who was puffing like a coon too full of fish. "I want that haunted stump," he said again. "That would really be something to take to school. Sandy said it was right by the cave's fireplace. Can I have it, Plum Nelly?"

Plum Nelly laughed so hard he knocked the potato bowl on the floor, and all the spuds he'd peeled went rolling every which way. One thumped against Yellow Dog Dingo's nose, making the surprised dog bat it with a paw as if it were a ball.

"So you want the haunted stump!" Plum Nelly roared with glee.

Kit didn't change his mind. "You bet I do," he said firmly through tight lips.

"You just think you do." Plum Nelly was as determined as Kit.

"I *know* I do," insisted the boy.

Sandy and his father were too amazed to say anything. They just couldn't understand Kit's wanting a piece of an old tree that had been burned out in some fire.

"Look here, Kit," Plum Nelly said finally. "You say you want a haunted stump, an' I say you don't. You'll be a lot better off if you forget Sandy saw that ugly, burned-out stump in the cave. I can guarantee that!" He scooped potatoes from the floor and stomped to the stove, banging pots and muttering "Great guns and pickled pigs' feet" under his breath.

Kit followed him. "Why don't I want it? Just tell me why."

"Because that stump is murder, that's why!" Plum Nelly glared down at the boy.

"Golly," put in Sandy, "maybe a haunted stump is a lot better than an old rifle and a powder flask, even if it is brass. I'll trade you, Kit."

Kit shook his head. "Nope, the stump is mine. You keep the gun—and the flask, too. Nobody's ever, ever taken a real haunted anything to school. But I'm going to."

"Well, well, well," said Plum Nelly. "I never seen such a hardheaded boy. You're more stubborn than Uncle Bert ever was. You're more stubborn than a mule. You sure are. I've got a mighty good notion—a *mighty* good one—jest to let you take that haunted stump an' see what happens. Yes, sir! That would teach you a lesson."

"What do you mean, Plum Nelly?" asked Mr. Duncan, who had been sitting quietly thinking that Plum Nelly was just teasing Kit. Now he wasn't so sure. "What do you mean, Plum Nelly?"

Plum Nelly turned. "I won't say right this minute," he sputtered. "Wait till I'm not so busy, an' I'll tell you the true story of the awful work done by the haunted stump."

He shook salt into a kettle and put the potatoes on to boil.

13 The Stump with Ghostly Hands

Plum Nelly slammed the potato pot on the stove. He wiped his hands on his trousers and stirred the fire into flame. Satisfied, he scraped peelings into the garbage bucket and turned to look long and searchingly at the anxious boys.

"You going to tell us now?" asked Kit, who could hardly wait. "You going to tell us about the haunted stump?"

"Yup," said Plum Nelly, "I guess so." But he didn't hurry. He set the garbage pail outside. Then he fussed around with his rocking chair, half sat down, hopped up to peer at the potatoes and see if they were boiling, peeked out the window, sat down again, and then bobbed up quick as a rabbit under a windfall and shot into the bunkroom.

Sandy frowned. "Now what's the matter with him?"

"I've learned," their father said quietly, "that there isn't any use hurrying Plum Nelly. He isn't the kind who can be rushed. Everything comes to him who waits, and Plum Nelly, when he sets his mind to it, can do a lot of making people wait. Here he comes now."

Plum Nelly came sauntering in as if he hadn't been in fidgets a minute before. "Thought of somethin' I wanted to look at," he said, settling down in the rocker. "Now, then—" he breathed deeply—"seems to me I wuz goin' to tell you about the haunted stump, wasn't I?"

"Yes," burst out both boys together.

"Well, then, you got to sit quietly. I can't stand people jumpin' 'round and actin' excited. It gerguzzleshabens me."

Sandy was puzzled. "It gerguzzle . . ." He gave it up and began again. "It does *what* to you, Plum Nelly?"

"It riles me," Plum Nelly said shortly. "Be quiet, will you, if you want to hear 'bout that derned stump."

"Oh, for heaven's sake," put in Mr. Duncan, who was as anxious as the boys, "you interrupt yourself more than the boys do."

Plum Nelly nodded agreeably. "Guess I do, at that. Comes from livin' alone so much—if a feller didn't interrupt himself now and then, he'd git bored. Sometimes I wish I wuz teaching school again, like when I was younger."

The boys sat up straight at hearing this. "I didn't know you taught school," exclaimed Kit, wonder filling his voice.

"There's lots of things you don't know," said Plum Nelly. His sharp eyes took in Sandy, who was rubbing the rifle with an oiled rag, and flickered to Kit, who sat on the floor with Yellow Dog Dingo's head in his lap.

"Well," he continued, "Sandy fumbled on that old cave in the rain and storm this afternoon, not knowin' it was a lumberjacks' hangout and a robbers' den. And not knowin', either, that early explorers from Canada made it their headquarters. I'd almost forgotten about it myself—it's been seven or eight years since I'd been up there. Bet there aren't more than a dozen folks in the county could find it. And if they could, they wouldn't want to—because of the stump that Sandy says is still hidin' there, waitin' and watchin' and plannin' to catch another victim.

"A long time ago, when this country was so young there wasn't more than three or four families around Broadwater Bay, the lumber companies bought acres of big trees and began sendin' crews in to cut. Men cut and chopped and sawed, and the trees kept fallin' down—thunderin' to earth like giants toppled from the sky.

"Pretty soon the woods were littered with cuttings and stumps standing alone and naked where once was a mighty forest. The land was left to new settlers who wanted to farm. They had to clean up the mess. It wasn't an easy job, no, sir!"

"How did they clean up, Plum Nelly?" Kit stopped petting Yellow Dog to ask the question.

"They had log-burnings, Kit. Folks from miles around

came for a neighbor's log-burning. It was sorta like a picnic. Everybody had a good time, but everybody worked, too. The preacher would come, wearin' overalls. And the doctor, if he wasn't busy, and the lawyer. Schoolteachers, blacksmiths, traders, trappers, and men runnin' for office—they all would be there. Maybe a few Chippewa Indians, too. They'd rake and burn and rake some more. They'd kindle big fires in the stumps, fires that glowed and ate away the tough wood all day. At night, flames lit up the sky and showered sparks in clouds. There'd be singin' and a keg of cider and red meat and laughin' and cuttin' up.

"Like I say, there wuz work for everybody. Even the women and girls tended stump fires, watchin' to see if they burned bright and pokin' in long poles to stir up the flames. That's when it happened, and so—"

"That's when what happened?" Sandy could never stop asking questions.

Plum Nelly kept right on talking as if Sandy hadn't opened his mouth.

"There wuz a log-burning near the bay here at the Jackson place. Emily Jackson was eighteen years old, and she was beautiful. Lots of golden hair she had, and pretty blue eyes and a smile for everyone. She was the apple of her father's eye. This night she had a pole and was pushin' log rubbish up against a smoldering stump—pushin' and laughin' with the boys and makin' jokes and callin' to her mother she'd be in to help with the refreshments in just a minute. Red-hot sparks flew from the stump, sprinklin' the air with fiery spots. Emily's eyes watered, and her cheeks got red from the heat. She laughed and pushed harder with her pole.

"Suddenly the pole caught in the stump. When she tried to jerk it out, she lost her balance. She toppled screaming into the blazing stump. Her pretty hands slid right into the white-hot fire. She screamed like a mink hung in a trap or an owl that feels steel jaws closing around its hooked claws. Everybody ran to help her—to pull her out.

"When they rescued her and laid her on the ground, with her mother running to fetch grease to put on her burns, they found that only her hands were hurt. But they were scorched and seared and shriveled into tight claws."

Plum Nelly stuck a fork into the potatoes, then settled himself in the rocker again.

"It was lucky—mighty lucky—the doctor had come to the burnin'. He said right away there was nothin' he could do but take off her poor shriveled hands. And he did, right then and there. He dropped Emily's hands straight into the fiery stump—the very one the girl fell into."

"Did she die, Plum Nelly?" Kit quavered.

"No, she didn't. She was sick a long time, though. Emily Jackson lived to be an old lady. All her life she used iron hooks for hands—doin' her washin' and cookin' and bakin' almost as well as any other woman. But she never went to another log-burning. Never. She's buried over in the family cemetery."

"But the stump—the stump in Sandy's cave. How did it get there?" Kit cried.

"I wuz comin' to that," said Plum Nelly. "For a long spell after Emily's accident, nobody would go near the stump. Maybe they couldn't stand thinkin' of the hurt it did Emily and the hands that were burned up in it.

They shunned the spot. The Chippewa said the Evil Spirit was there. After a few years people began to forgit, the way folks generally do. So they ventured near. And some came back with pretty strange tales. They'd tell about two pale hands rising up out of the stump and beckoning to them, hands that wavered and shook. Nobody would believe such goings-on at first, but more and more saw 'em. Sometimes the hands wouldn't be white and pale at all, but red and black. Only the bones that stuck out were white—not glossy-white like the patches on Yellow Dog Dingo's fur, but ghost-white, and ghost-white's got gray in it. Death's gray.

"After a time, the hands, all ghost-white, came out of the stump to stir the air and do what looked like dancin'. At night folks that went anywhere near the stump felt hands on their shoulders or touchin' their faces light as a shadow, but feelin' sticky and crawly. Like cobwebs. And every time this happened, a smell came up in the night air. A smell of burning wood and flesh."

"That's a lot of bunk, Plum Nelly," Sandy said positively. "It couldn't happen. Folks just imagined those ghost hands. That's what happened."

Plum Nelly thought a long minute, sitting back in the rocker and closing his eyes. Then he said, "I guess maybe you're right, Sandy. It couldn't happen." He paused. "But the funny thing about it is that it did!" He went on. "The hand-claws of the haunted stump reached for strangers who'd never heard of Emily Jackson's accident. Let me tell you 'bout a newcomer on his way to work up near Walker. Walker was just a little town then and not the county seat like it is now. This stranger's name was

Jensen or Andersen or Peterson or Swenson or somethin'
foreign like that. I sort of forgit his right name now. It
don't make no difference, because he was dead soon after
they found him, and wouldn't have use for a name any
more.

"This Petersen or Swenson or whatever his name was
stopped in town one night for supper and said he was
looking for work at Walker, like I said. He wanted to
know if there was a short cut, because he didn't like to
walk any more than necessary. Somebody told him to cut
through the farm of Emily Jackson's father. And off he
went, head high like he owned the world and was goin'
to live forever.

"About an hour later, Ole Man Jackson heard yells and
screams comin' from near the stump. He ran out, and
here was the stranger flopping on the ground and tossin'
like he couldn't get a breath. 'I'm chokin,' yells the
stranger. 'There's hands around my throat.' Jackson ran
over, lifted the man up, and felt his neck. He touched a
pair of hands 'round the stranger's neck. Ole Man Jackson couldn't see the hands, but he felt 'em! After the
stranger died, there right on his neck were red marks of
two sets of fingers. The hands had come out of the
haunted stump to do murder.

"The sheriff didn't arrest Jackson or even suspect him,
because he knew who'd done the stranger in—the old evil
stump still hot with hate. Some new folks in the county
always thought Jackson did it, but there wasn't any proof,
and anyhow, Jackson had never seen the stranger before,
so why would he have strangled him? And Jackson was a
slight old man, too feeble to choke anybody. Like I said

once, Sandy, there's queer things happen in the woods."

Sandy didn't know what to say to that, but he had a question. "Plum Nelly, how did that terrible stump get into my cave?"

Plum Nelly sighed. "I put it there," he said finally.

"Then it's yours," cried Kit, pushing Yellow Dog Dingo's head off his lap and coming to stand by the rocking chair. "You own the stump with the ghostly hands."

"Nobody owns it," said Plum Nelly shortly, "unless it be the devil."

"But why did you take it to the cave? And didn't it hurt you?" Sandy couldn't understand this at all.

"I'll tell you how it was," said Plum Nelly, "but I wouldn't want the neighbors to know I did it. It happened this way. After the stranger was strangled on Jackson's farm, things went from bad to worse. Even the wild animals wouldn't feed on his land. Deer avoided the place. Bears and wolves skirted around it. Even ducks and geese wouldn't fly over it. Why, things got so bad I had to hunt ducks with pumpkins one year, and just because of that stump."

"Just a minute, Plum Nelly," said Mr. Duncan. "Nobody ever shot ducks with pumpkins."

"I didn't say I did. I said I *hunted* ducks with pumpkins. There's a difference," said Plum Nelly.

"Well, what do you mean?" Mr. Duncan settled himself more comfortably.

"I mean this, jest this," said Plum Nelly. "Like I said, it got so hunting was mighty poor. The deer stayed away, and the ducks were so scary they'd fly at the drop of a hat. Nervous-like, they were. Wouldn't light but fer a few minutes and then up they'd go again, circling 'round like crazy. That's why I hunted them with pumpkins."

"There you go again," said Mr. Duncan.

"There I don't go again," bellowed Plum Nelly. "I'm tryin' to tell yuh, and all you do is make silly remarks. You gerguzzleshabens me, you do!" He snorted in disgust and made a great to-do about putting more wood in the stove, although the fire was steady and purring like a tame cat.

When he calmed down and was in his rocker again, Plum Nelly resumed. "I knew the ghost stump was frightening all game away, and there's nothin' I like better than roast duck. But the birds wouldn't settle long enough for me to shoot 'em, and they were flyin' too high to knock 'em off in the air. I wuz desperate and gettin' hungrier by the day for duck. Then I thought of something. I remembered how they used to light in the pumpkin patch. I got a big pumpkin, big enough fer me to get my head in, and I hollowed it out, leaving a big hole in the bottom. One morning early, before the birds came across the lake, I waded in until the water came up to my neck. Then I slipped the hollow pumpkin over my head. It looked like it wuz jest floatin' there on the water. Well, boys, those ducks jest made for the pumpkin, floatin' all innocent-like. They spread their wings and settled down all around it, flappin' and talkin' duck talk and paddlin' 'round. All I had to do was reach out, grab 'em by the legs, and pull 'em under. I got me a whole mess of ducks in about fifteen minutes that way. But it was mighty cold standin' neck-deep in lake water in October, and I didn't relish it much.

No, sir. I decided the easiest thing to do was to get rid of the stump so it wouldn't scare game away. Then I could go back to huntin' natural and proper-like."

"Weren't you scared to move the stump?" asked Kit, peering earnestly into Plum Nelly's face.

"You bet I was! But it had to be done."

Kit moved slowly away from Plum Nelly, keeping his eyes on him all the while, and sat down on the floor again close to Yellow Dog Dingo. Then he said slowly, "How did you dare move it?"

"Once I started, it wasn't so bad. First I got a heavy log chain and fastened one end to a team of horses I had then. This was long before I had the jeep, you know. I drove out to the stump right at noon, when ghosts are weakest, of a bright, sunny day. Quick as a flash I circled the haunted stump with the chain. The horses stood quiet enough until the chain went around. Then, just like a bolt of lightnin' had hit 'em, they begun to quiver and buck and neigh. They lit out, runnin' like Old Scratch was after 'em. I had all I could do to keep up, but I turned 'em toward the cave and rolled the stump in. I noticed it was getting hotter and hotter all the time and sendin' out little puffs of smoke that smelled like sulphur. Then the chain snapped, and gave me this."

Plum Nelly peeled back his sleeve. A long scar twisted up his arm. It was red and so vicious-looking that it seemed fresh instead of old. Running a finger along it, Plum Nelly said, "That's why I don't venture into the cave no more than I have to. I dunno when that evil stump worked itself way back there where Sandy saw it."

"Did moving the stump help hunting, Plum Nelly?" said Sandy, who could hardly keep his gaze from the scar that the stump had made.

"Well, I'll tell yuh," answered Plum Nelly, rolling down his sleeve. "No sooner wuz that stump out of the way than the deer came back and the bears, and the ducks and geese began settin' down on the potholes and the lake again. Never have had any trouble getting my limit since."

"Plum Nelly," Kit said earnestly, "if it's all right with you, I don't think I want to take that mean, haunted stump back to school with me. It better stay where it is."

"I reckon that's smart, son—the haunted stump with the ghostly hands better stay right there in Sandy's cave. I wouldn't even talk about it any more if I wuz you."

Kit shuddered. "I don't even want to think about it."

"And I," added Sandy, "never, never want to go back to the cave."

14 Search for the Golden Minnow

"Time to feed the Indians!"

Both boys jumped. "Indians! What Indians, Plum Nelly?"

"Why, my Indians. Right over there—see 'em?" Plum Nelly pointed through the window. The boys craned their necks.

"Are they hiding?" Sandy peered under Plum Nelly's arm. "I don't see them. Will they come in?"

"I don't see anything, either," said Kit.

"Great guns and pickled pigs' feet," shouted Plum Nelly. "There they are—fifty or more—in red paint right this side of the barn."

The boys looked again, their eyes following Plum Nelly's pointer finger. There stood the barn, all right, and the jeep and the icehouse. Everything looked just as it did each morning. There wasn't a brave in war paint anywhere. Sandy's sharp eyes even searched the trees and scanned the lake shore for canoes.

Plum Nelly still pointed. "They come every year jest 'bout this time."

"But Plum Nelly," Kit said anxiously, "there aren't any Indians out there. You sick or something? I don't see a thing but a flock of robins."

A big laugh roared out of Plum Nelly. "That's what I mean. The robins are the Indians."

"Now I'm sure he's sick," whispered Kit to Sandy. "You better call Dad. Maybe he ate too many doughnuts."

Sandy edged away to call Mr. Duncan, but Plum Nelly shot out a hand and twirled him back. "Some folks see only with their eyes," he said, "but in the woods you have to use your eyes and your head." He turned, looking hard at the bewildered boys. "See what I mean?"

They shook their heads. Plum Nelly didn't seem to make sense a lot of the time. If he thought robins were Indians, there must be something wrong with him.

"Oh, I know what you're thinking," said Plum Nelly, "and it isn't so. I'm not sick. You see robins, and I see robins and Indians." The boys nodded. They certainly did see birds, but they couldn't understand why Plum Nelly thought they were Indians.

"Plum Nelly," Kit said firmly, "why do you think those robins are Indians?"

The guide laughed. "Just wait till I take a pan of crumbs to those feathered warriors, and I'll tell you. They're gittin' ready to go south fer the winter, and I'm no one to send 'em away without a good meal."

Kit and Sandy watched Plum Nelly toss cake crumbs and toast crusts and a few snips of dry bread to the hungry birds. His lips moved, but they couldn't understand what he said. It looked as though the robins knew, for they cocked their heads and acted for all the world as if their chittering were conversation.

"Do you suppose they really are talking?" Sandy wanted to know.

"I dunno—here he comes now." Kit opened the door for Plum Nelly and the empty pan.

"Now then," said Plum Nelly, "I've got 'em fed and they're properly thankful, they are. Count on me every fall to give 'em a bite." He turned to the boys. "So you think I'm crazy because my robins are Indians, do yuh?"

"Well, not exactly," Kit stammered, "but I don't understand how—"

"I know, I know," said Plum Nelly. "You don't understand how Indians can be robins."

"That's not it, Plum Nelly," Sandy answered. "We don't understand how robins can be Indians."

"You've got it twisted, lad. Robins were Indians before they were robins." The boys were so confused that Plum Nelly felt sorry for them. "Remember I told you a woodsman had to see with more than his eyes?" The boys looked blank. "It's this way," Plum Nelly began patiently.

"When you see a track in the woods it's jest a pattern on the ground, isn't it? You've got ter know in your head if it's a bear track or a deer track or an old porcupine draggin' his tail."

"That's right," Kit said. "Isn't it, Sandy?" Sandy nodded, but he still couldn't quite see what Plum Nelly was driving at.

"Now then," Plum Nelly said, "there's heaps of things a man jest has to know. Take those robins, fer instance. I call 'em Indians 'cause I know how they came to be. Yes, sir, I know."

"How did they come to be?" asked Sandy.

"It was this way," Plum Nelly went on. "This is the way the Ojibwa believed it happened a very long time ago. A long time ago, so the story goes, there was a brave warrior who had an only son. The boy's name was Opeechee. He was a good boy, a little older than Kit here. He liked to snare the long-eared rabbit, to follow the prints of the deer, to fish with hand-woven line. His arrows flew true to the mark. Opeechee was a good boy, and his father was very proud of him.

"In a land of many lakes and in the big forests, Opeechee's father taught the boy the ways of the wilderness—taught him to understand the loon's laugh, to dry fish in the sun, to know the healing herbs. When he was older and had learned all he could, it was time for Opeechee to be a man.

"Opeechee's father took him to the sweating lodge, where water poured over hot rocks steamed and cleaned the boy. Then he was led to a tepee set away from all others and told to rest upon a mat of sweet grasses. Opee-

chee was to lie there for twelve days without food. Only a little jug of water was within reach. Sometime during the twelve days a vision would come to Opeechee. He would know from the vision what he should do as a man, whether he would be a great chief or a mighty warrior. When Opeechee stretched himself on the mat, close to the water jug, his father left him alone, being careful to fasten the lodge's door flap of deer hide.

"Opeechee waited and waited for the vision. On the ninth day a shadowy figure stood by his side. The figure, in full war dress and with face crisscrossed with the black paint of evil things to come, warned the boy that no good was in store for him and told him to break his fast and to come again to the lodge of manhood when another twelve moons had passed.

"That day, when Opeechee's father visited him, the boy told what the vision had said and asked his father if he might break the fast and make another in the new year. But the father answered that he must go on, saying another vision would appear.

"Opeechee wept and again lay down. On the eleventh day, when no new vision had come, he pleaded with his father to let him give up the fast. But the old man again told him he must go on, that it was for his own good. The boy pulled his robe over his head and lay motionless as the dead."

Plum Nelly paused to put match to his pipe. Kit and Sandy never took their eyes from his face. What was going to happen to Opeechee?

"On the twelfth and last day of the fast in the lodge," said Plum Nelly, blowing out the match, "the father again came to the lodge of manhood. He pulled aside the deer-skin flap covering the door. As he stooped to enter, he heard Opeechee talking to himself. But the father was even more surprised to see his son painting vermilion over his breast and laying it down his back as far as hands could reach. The father heard Opeechee cry out, 'My father has destroyed my fortune as a man. He would not let me obey the vision, but my vision has showed pity for me. He is giving me a new shape, and now I must go.' Then the father, frightened, exclaimed, 'My son! My son! I pray you not to go!'

"But the young man, with the quickness of a bird, flew to the top of the lodge and perched himself on the highest pole. Opeechee was changed into a beautiful robin redbreast. He looked with pity at his father. 'Do not grieve, my parent. I shall be happier than if I were a man. I shall always be a friend to man and live near his home and sing for him and cheer him with my songs; and I shall be among the first birds to come back to man in the spring and among the last to leave him in the autumn.' Then Opeechee stretched himself on his toes, sang a new sweet song, and flew away. This is why robins are Indians," said Plum Nelly as he finished his story.

Kit and Sandy sat silent. Even Plum Nelly did not stir. He was watching the robins, fluttering and worm-digging, the first to come back in the spring and the last to leave in the fall. He was noting their gay red breasts, their saucy heads, and their bright, friendly eyes.

Sandy walked to the window. "Plum Nelly," he asked, "do you really believe those robins are Opeechee's children? Do you, Plum Nelly?"

"Yes, son." Plum Nelly turned around. "I reckon I do."

Sandy's face took on puzzled wrinkles. His mouth opened and closed, but no sound came. He looked searchingly at Plum Nelly, started to speak, then turned away. "Come on, Yellow Dog Dingo," he called, "I'll race you to the dock."

"Wait a minute!" Kit motioned Sandy back. "Come here, Sandy, we've forgotten something."

"What's that?"

"We haven't opened the secret panel," answered Kit. Yellow Dog Dingo flopped down on the floor, yawned, and stretched his nose between his paws.

"Let's see what it says for today." Sandy snatched the slip of paper when the tiny door swung open. Kit peeked over his shoulder.

"It says," Sandy read, "to find the treasure at the Sign of . . . at the Sign of The Golden Minnow."

"The Sign of the Golden Minnow!" Kit grabbed the paper. "Now, what is a gold minnow? Will you tell me that?"

Sandy shrugged. "Can't you keep your mouth shut?" he said. "There's something else, if you'd only take time to read it." He snatched the slip from Kit. "See, it says to look first in the icehouse."

The boys flew out the door so fast it banged shut on Yellow Dog Dingo's nose. He wanted to go along, and he howled and scratched until Plum Nelly let him out. Yellow Dog Dingo caught up with the boys before they reached the dim, cool icehouse.

"I don't see any gold minnow," Kit said, looking all around.

"Me neither." Sandy was sliding and slithering over the sawdust covering the ice cakes. "Do you suppose Plum Nelly's got a gold minnow in his magic tackle box?"

"He could have anything. Him with his Indians and his robins!" Kit shivered. "Say, it's cold in here—let's get out." The words were hardly said before his feet shot from under him and he tumbled headlong to crash against a heavy timbered wall.

"Kit! Kit! Are you hurt?"

Kit rolled over on all four feet and hands and shook himself as a dazed bear does when he comes from his winter's sleep. He blinked, closed his eyes, winked them open again, and stood up. "Wow," he said, "that ice sure is slippery." He felt his head and shook himself again. "I guess I'm all right, but I wouldn't want to do that every day. Come on, Sandy, let's get—" He never finished, for his face took on a strange look and his eyes stared.

Sandy was frightened. For a moment he was more worried than he had been when he got lost and found the old cave and the rifle and the powder flask and the horrible haunted stump. He thought Kit was having a fit. Sandy was ready to run for help when Kit choked out, "There it is—there it is." He scrambled up the ice pile again, making sawdust fly.

Then Sandy saw it: a small sign, shaped like a minnow, nailed to the wall. Yanking it down, Kit brought it to Sandy. "Bro-*ther*, does my head hurt! Read what's written on it, Sandy; I'm going to sit down."

"You sure you're all right?" Sandy asked anxiously.

"I'm going to be all right. Just don't stand there and look at me. Read what it says."

"Well, you don't have to get so mad just because you banged your head. I'll read it. It says we're to smell where the mint grows tall. What does that mean, do you suppose?"

"I know, I know," Kit answered, forgetting to rub his head. "Plum Nelly showed me the other day. Come on!"

He darted out the icehouse door, ran behind the barn, and circled the vegetable garden. He dropped on his knees and pawed through a mint clump. Yellow Dog Dingo thought it was a game and started to dig, sending dirt and mint plants flying. "You stop that, Dingo, right now!" Kit yanked the dog away. "Now sit down there and stay, I tell you." Poor Yellow Dog Dingo sat on his haunches with pink tongue lolling. If Kit could dig, why shouldn't he?

"Here's another one, Sandy, but it's all dirty."

"What does it say?"

"Umph, that's funny." Kit brushed off more dirt. "This one says: 'Where there's a well, there's a way.' I can't understand it. Whoever wrote it can't spell—he means where there's a *will*, there's a way. Now what do we do?"

Sandy didn't answer. He was thinking hard. With the ache in his head and the mystery that faced him, Kit was content to rest and wait for Sandy's ideas. He pulled a sprig of mint. It smelled clean, and the taste cooled his mouth. When he pinched a leaf between his fingers for Yellow Dog Dingo to sniff, the hound's wet nose nuzzled his hand. "It does smell good," the boy said. Dingo's tail wagged "yes."

"Kit?"

"What?"

"What does 'Where there's a will, there's a way' mean?"

Kit chewed hard on the mint. "Well," he said, "I guess it means that when a fellow wants to do something bad enough, he can."

"I want to find the golden minnow."

"So do I," Kit replied, "but 'where there's a will, there's a way' doesn't tell us where to look next. The first clue in the icehouse told us to find the wild mint. This doesn't tell us anything." Kit rubbed the bump on his head.

"Maybe it does," Sandy said suddenly.

"Maybe it does what?"

Sandy was excited. "Maybe it does tell us where to look. Maybe it means what it says, Kit!"

"What do you mean?"

"I think it means to look where there's a well." Sandy was pleased with himself.

"A well?" Kit repeated stupidly.

"Sure, a well—a place to get water. Plum Nelly's got an old well. It's where he used to get water before Uncle Bert put in the pump."

Kit's face lit up. "Maybe you've got something there. I bet Plum Nelly thought he was tricking us. Where's that old well, Sandy?"

"I'll show you—it's near the barn in a weed patch. Come on!"

No two boys ever ran faster than Kit and Sandy. Yellow Dog Dingo followed, barking louder than when the skunk sprayed him.

The planks covering the abandoned well were overgrown with creepers—a tangled mess for the boys to pull away—and the weeds smelled strong and sour, not like the cool fragrance of the mint.

"Watch those planks," Kit warned as Sandy plunged headlong into the vine tangle. "Don't fall through."

"I don't have to. I've got it—the sign's right here." Sandy backed out, holding the third minnow-shaped clue. "We sure fooled old Plum Nelly this time. I bet he never thought we'd figure out that 'will' and 'well' business."

"I bet he didn't, either," Kit chuckled. "What does this one say?"

"Golly, it's a long one. There's a lot of writing."

"I'll read it." Kit grabbed the sign. It said: *A punt and a phew and a point, and there's the Sign of the Golden Minnow.*

"A punt and a phew and a point," Sandy repeated. "Kit, I can't even guess what it means. Plum Nelly's got us licked this time."

"Well, I know what a punt is," Kit said firmly. "It's a kind of boat." Then he added, "But I don't know what a 'phew' is."

"Mother says 'phew' when something smells just awful," Sandy suggested.

"And you said 'phew' and held your nose when Dingo tangled with the skunk."

"I guess I did. And you know, Plum Nelly says the same thing when he rows over to the point in the lake."

Kit nodded. "I know he does. He always— Hey, wait a minute! It's Pew's Point the sign's talking about, and Plum Nelly wrote it wrong just to throw us off, like when he wanted us to think 'well' was 'will.' We've got it now. We're going to Pew's Point!"

"But," Sandy protested, "we can't take the boat without asking. Plum Nelly said we couldn't go out on the lake without his permission."

"All right, then, we'll ask him."

Plum Nelly watched the boys hurry up the path. He pretended to be busy when they rushed in, shouting they wanted to use the boat. He said he might want to go fishing and would need the boat. It was too late in the morning to go out on the lake. When he saw the lump on Kit's head, Plum Nelly insisted on pressing a cold knife to it to make it feel better. He said Kit ought to rest until he felt better. He hemmed and hawed and sputtered enough to drive the boys crazy.

"Great guns and pickled pigs' feet, why do you want to go out in a boat now?"

"Because," said Kit.

"Because," answered Sandy

"Because, because, because!" shouted Plum Nelly. "Why can't you stay here?"

"Because," said Sandy.

And Kit repeated, "Because."

Plum Nelly collapsed in a chair, pretending he was tuckered out with all the silly talk. He took his pipe out of his mouth and hid his face in his hands. When the boys spoke to him he wouldn't answer. Only little disgusted moans and chirrups came out. Finally one eye peeked through his fingers. "Well," he mumbled, "if you must go, all right. But you'll have to row. I've got the motor in the boathouse and I'm not a-goin' to put it on for two 'because' boys. Now git!"

"I bet he took the motor off on purpose," Kit grumbled when the boys untied the boat. "You get in first, Sandy, and grab the oars. I'll shove off—and be careful you don't bang the dock."

Woman Lake never was more beautiful. A bright sun danced reflections from the water. On every shore and inlet pines stood tall and straight. The only noise was the gurgle of water under Sandy's oars.

"You know," said Kit, "I'd like to come back again—just this time of year."

"So would I," Sandy said, "but we're usually in school. We'd be there now if there wasn't a teachers' convention. How far is it now?"

"Only a little ways," Kit answered. "Pull on the right oar more. Want me to help? I'm not tired."

"Nope, there's no wind and the rowing's easy. How's your head?"

Kit felt the tender lump. "It's better, I guess. Plum Nelly's cold knife helped. Here we are. Give her a couple of big pulls, Sandy, and she'll slide up the beach."

Sandy pulled as hard as he could, and the boat grated over pebbles and slid to rest on smooth sand. They tied it to a tree and scrambled out on Pew's Point.

"Well, we're here," said Sandy, rubbing tired arms. "Now what do we do?"

"The clue didn't say what to do after we got here."

"There'll be a sign. I know it." Sandy was confident.

Pew's Point was not much more than a thick thumb sticking out in the lake near a narrows. On the side where the boys landed stretched a sandy, shelving beach, but the side near the narrows was shallow and grown up with reeds. Beyond these, in deeper water, lived big-mouthed bass. Here were Plum Nelly's favorite bass grounds. A few hundred yards on was the entrance to Boy Lake, and on beyond that stood the crumbling remains of an old logging bridge. Its decaying piles were the home of sunfish. The point itself bristled with shoulder-high underbrush. Only a few puny pines grew there.

"This will be a tough place to find anything," said Kit, pushing through brush that snapped against his legs and caught his hair.

"What do you suppose a gold minnow is?" Sandy pushed along behind Kit, dodging brush branches.

"I dunno, but it better be good for all this work."

"It will be. I know it will." A branch raked Sandy's cheek. "Wow! that hurt!"

"So does my head," his brother grunted.

Pushing through the underbrush, the boys stepped out on the far side of the point, where the reedy narrows lay smooth as blue glass in the bright sun. No breeze reached this spot, and the reed spears stood motionless. On one stalk a bit of white flashed.

"What's that?" said Kit and Sandy in the same breath. Another look, and they saw a piece of paper fastened to a reed some distance from shore. There was no mistaking what it was.

Before Sandy realized what Kit was doing, he had pulled his shirt over his head and slipped out of his jeans. "I'm going to leave my sneakers on," he cried, wading into the water. "I don't want any old catfish stinging me."

Step by cautious step, Kit edged toward the paper. He had almost reached it when suddenly his feet slipped on the mucky bottom and he spilled head over heels. The splash sounded like a grandpappy bass jumping after a fat frog. Kit scrambled up, shook his head, spit a spray of water, and caught hold of the paper.

"Don't get it wet," Sandy warned.

Kit grinned. "Not a chance—I've had my bath for to-day."

"Oh, my gosh!" Sandy smoothed the note while Kit shook himself. "Did you bring your compass?"

"Of course I did. Why?"

"I forgot mine again, and we're going to need one."

Kit got into pants and shirt. "Mine's right here in my pocket. Why do you want it?"

"Because the note says to go forty-five feet due west from the reed where you got the paper, then fifteen feet northwest, and then seventy-five feet south, and then it says to dig where there's a split boulder."

"Umph," said Kit. He began to shuck off his clothes again. "You got any string?"

"No—and what's the idea of undressing? You just got them back on. Are you crazy or something?"

"Look, stupid. We got to measure from the reed to shore, and how are we going to do that without string and without me wading out there again? We can step off distance on land, but we've got to use string or something between that reed and the shore here. Understand?"

"But Kit, we haven't got any—"

Kit snapped his fingers. "Yes we have—we've got something just as good. There's some old fishline in the boat. Go get it, will you?"

"Okay, okay, but I don't see why I have to do all the work. I rowed over, remember?"

"I remember, and do you remember that I waded out and fell in the lake and that I hit my head in the icehouse? You can do something!"

"I'll get it," Sandy said meekly.

When he came back with the line, Kit took it and knotted one end to a stick. "Now, Sandy," he said, "you hold this end, and I'll wade out with the other. When I get there we'll stretch the line tight, and you mark the place where it touches the shore. Then we'll know how far it is. The rest will be easy."

Kit's plan worked perfectly. The fishline stretched straight and tight between Sandy on shore and Kit knee-deep in water at the reed. As soon as Kit had waded back, the boys paced off the line's length. It measured twenty-two feet—maybe a little more, perhaps a little less. "Let's see now," said Kit, who was better at arithmetic, "twenty-two from forty-five feet is twenty-three feet. We want to go twenty-three feet due west."

Sandy held the compass on true west, and Kit carefully paced off the distance. The next fifteen feet northwest were easy with the compass's help. An abrupt turn, and Kit counted seventy-five feet directly south. And there, in front of the boys, lay a broken boulder, split by time and weather. Here, at last, was the promised treasure—the

golden minnow whose trail ran from the icehouse to the
mint bed, from there to Plum Nelly's old well, and from
the well to Pew's Point.

Kit and Sandy knew where to dig, for the ground at the
rock's base on the north lay piled in an uneven mound.
"There's something under here, all right." Kit made the
earth fly. "I feel it, too," said Sandy. The soft ground gave
up its secret easily, and the boys lifted out a square tin
box. On its top was painted a gold minnow.

Two pairs of hands lifted the lid. Light flashed from inside, almost blinding the lads with it brilliance. The sun
shone on gold and silver, sending out sharp stabs of brightness. Sandy squinted to see the better, and Kit shaded his
eyes with one hand.

"It's a whole set of gold and silver lures!" Kit gasped.
"There's trolling spoons and—"

"—and wigglers and artificial minnows!" added Sandy.
"Kit, they're wonderful."

"Boy, wait till the kids at home see this!" Kit lifted a
casting bait with a silver head, black body, and golden tail.
"Oh bro-*ther*, did you ever see such a collection? I bet
you Plum Nelly had them made special for us. Dad hasn't
got anything like this."

"There's nothing like it in Plum Nelly's magic tackle
box, either," said Sandy. "If we can't catch fish now, nobody can. Come on, Sandy, let's start home. I can hardly
wait to show them off. We sure found the golden minnow
—we sure did!"

Kit really put his back to the oars, yet Sandy kept urging
him to row faster. The tin box, packed with marvelous
shining lures, he held on his lap. Sandy tilted the lid. Yes,

they were there, all right—each and every beautiful one of them. Their burnished bodies tossed off light reflections brighter than before, now that the boat swung from shore. The sun beat down from directly overhead. Sandy knew their value well enough. He had shopped with his father in sporting-goods stores too many times not to recognize that he and Kit now owned finer equipment than most fishermen.

"There's Plum Nelly and Dad on the dock." Sandy's head jerked and he grabbed the tie rope.

"Great guns and pickled pigs' feet," roared Plum Nelly a few minutes later, grabbing the rope and bringing the boat alongside. "So you found the golden minnow, did you?"

"We sure did," Kit shipped oars and stepped out. "Hand me the box, Sandy."

Up went the box, with Sandy scrambling after. "Plum Nelly, they're swell—gosh, they're super wonderful. Where did you get them?"

"Yes, where, Plum Nelly?" Kit put in, opening the box so his father could look.

"Where did I get them? Well, where do you think?"

"In the city?" Sandy asked.

"Or from a catalogue?" guessed Kit, examining a redheaded lure with golden back.

A smile creased Plum Nelly's face. "Not in the city and not from a catalogue."

"Then where? They're beautiful."

"I made 'em," Plum Nelly said smugly.

"You didn't!" Sandy just couldn't believe such perfect lures came from Plum Nelly's workshop.

"Yup," repeated Plum Nelly. "I made 'em with my

own hands. Took me most of all last winter, but your dad said you boys would be coming up here one of these times, and I wanted you to take something really nice back home with you."

"But you've given us so much—the compass and all."

Plum Nelly didn't seem to hear Kit. At any rate, he didn't answer. "Look here." He fingered in the box. "Here's a leetle feller for a fly rod, an' here's one that will jest fit a spinning outfit, and those big ones there—why, you'll catch the big muskies trolling with them. Each and every one of 'em balances perfectly, they do. I saw to that," he added pridefully.

"You're skilled with your hands, all right," Mr. Duncan told Plum Nelly.

"I've had to be—there isn't much I haven't worked at. But, pshaw, I kin do better'n that. You oughter see the stuff I turned out when I was young and these old fingers weren't as stiff." Plum Nelly caught the boys by the elbows, swung them around, and pushed them toward the cabin. "Sometimes I talk too danged much," he muttered to Mr. Duncan. "Boys don't care 'bout what happened a long time ago. Fill the woodbox," he called after the boys.

"Sure, Plum Nelly."

No woodbox ever was filled fuller or more carefully. Kit brought in big pieces, and Sandy carried little ones. First they laid a layer of kindling, then a layer of heavier stuff, and then another layer of kindling. So it went, layer by layer, until the very top of the top. And on this the boys placed a basket of shavings so tinder dry that each little piece, Kit boasted, would catch at the mere thought of fire.

"We can't make golden minnows, but we sure can pile wood," the boys told Plum Nelly.

"We-ell," Plum Nelly admitted cautiously, "you sure did all right today. It's too bad you're goin' home tomorrow. Wood-pilers like you I could use all winter."

"I don't like winter." Sandy was positive.

"And I don't want to go back to school. Why can't teachers' meetings last—" Kit struggled for an idea—"why can't they last from October to June? That would be great. Oh, boy!"

Plum Nelly had a ready answer. "It jest can't, that's all— it jest can't. We can't do without winter and without school. I didn't get a chance at schoolin' till I wuz about grown up. You boys are lucky. Nope, winter is a part of nature. Oh, I ain't blamin' you fer not lookin' forward to it. The Chippewa have a saying that every warrior weeps within himself when winter comes, but his tears form the pools that freshen the springtime and bring leaf buds and flowers. I'll tell you a story 'bout winter if you want to hear it."

"If it's a real, true story," Kit said.

"Sit down, then, and I'll tell it to you as I heard it. I was trapping up on the Bow String just this time of year, when the leaves were coloring and falling and a wind blowed down from the north, tossing pine tops and puffing red spurts from the campfire. An old Ojibwa chief, with a face like a wrinkled prune, told me the story. You know, Ojibwa is another name for Chippewa—"

"Opeechee was Ojibwa, wasn't he, Plum Nelly?" Sandy asked.

"Yup, Ojibwa or Chippewa, it's all the same. Well, this old chief and me was talkin' 'bout winter, and I said how cold it was and how long it was and wished there never was winter. The chief, he kept nodding his head, agreeing with my complaints, but at the end, when I said I wished there never was winter, he scowled and told me about the way his people felt. I'll tell it to you the way he told it to me."

This is the story Kit and Sandy heard Plum Nelly tell: The leaves were gone and the cold had come. The north country lay blanketed with silent snow. Furry animals slept in their dens, and trees trembled and cracked in the wind. Alone in his lodge by the side of a frozen stream sat an old man. His fire was so tiny it gave almost no warmth, so that the man trembled and combed his long beard with shaking fingers. One day, when the last stick burned in the fire and a howling, wind-driven storm covered the lodge with snow, a young man pushed aside the flap and entered the lodge. He was so young his cheeks showed pink, his eyes sparkled, his lips were full and red. The old man saw a bunch of flowers in his hand.

"Come in, my son," said the old one, making room near the flickering fire. "I will tell you of my life, and you tell me of yours." They packed a pipe with sweet kinnikinnick and passed it one to another, each blowing a puff to the four winds. Then they told of their great deeds.

"I blow my breath," boasted the old man, "and rivers and streams and tiny creeks stand still. The water becomes still and hard as stone."

"When I breathe, flowers spring up and laugh," said the young stranger.

The old man said, "When I shake my gray beard, snow covers the land. Leaves fall from trees at my command, and my breath blows them away. The birds get up early and fly to a distant land. The animals hide themselves in their dens, and the very ground is hard as flint."

"I shake my curly hair," said the young warrior, "to make warm rain fall on the earth and soften it. Then the plants lift up their heads from out of the ground. My voice brings the birds back from the southland, and the warmth of my breath unlocks the streams that are as still and hard as stones. This is what I do."

With this speech the sun came up and a gentle warmth filled the lodge. A robin sang, and a bluebird flashed bright wings. Even the stream by the lodge unlocked itself and murmured softly and ran with the delight of its freedom. Flowers and ferns pushed through the earth. As the sun shone brighter, the old man grew smaller, melting away until, at last, he disappeared. Nothing was left where his lodge had once stood but a white flower with a pink border.

"Even the Chippewa knew that all nature must sleep and rest a part of the year," said Plum Nelly when the tale was over. "And they knew that spring always follows winter."

"Well, I guess winter's okay," said Sandy, "but I bet the Chippewa never told you a story about how good school is."

"I never heard one," admitted Plum Nelly, "but don't get the idea Indian boys don't have to learn. They do, and their lessons are mighty hard."

"Gee, Plum Nelly," Kit said admiringly, "you know a lot, don't you?"

Plum Nelly grinned. "Not as much as sometimes I think I do. You better begin to pack if you're goin' home tomorrow. I've got chores ter do."

15 *The Secret Panel's*

Last Secret

Getting ready to go on a vacation is fun, but packing to go home makes a boy's heart heavy.

Nobody knew this better than Kit and Sandy. Their long, sad faces and quiet tongues showed the grief they felt. Kit sat down to breakfast with a dirty face; and Sandy, who was always hungry, only toyed with Plum Nelly's golden pancakes.

"What's the matter with you two?" demanded Plum Nelly. "Here's a fresh batch of cakes, an' you haven't cleaned up the first." He tilted Sandy's chin. "You," he went on, "don't you like my cookin', or are you sick or somethin'? Great guns and pickled pigs' feet, these here are my best cakes!"

Sandy nodded. "I know they are, Plum Nelly, but . . . but I'm just not hungry." His voice quavered so that Plum Nelly took a long, searching look.

"Hmph," he said. "Guess maybe I know how you feel. But it's nothing a good breakfast won't fix. Now, you and Kit clean up these flapjacks. No woodsman can go to town on an empty belly."

"But, Plum Nelly," Kit protested, "we aren't going to town—we're going home today and back to school."

"Sure you are, an' it's the best thing could happen to yuh!"

Sandy looked sadder than ever. "Something got in my eye," he said, brushing away what might have been a tear. He blew his nose hard. "I'm just not hungry, Plum Nelly."

"Sure you're hungry, an' you're goin' to eat those cakes or I'm a-goin' to push 'em into you. I mean it," warned Plum Nelly, spearing a pancake and thrusting it at the wet-eyed boy.

A mouth opened automatically, and in went the cake. Sandy just had to chew, and when he chewed, sweet maple syrup dribbled down his chin. The cakes were good, there was no doubt about it. He gulped bravely and yanked the fork from Plum Nelly. "I guess I'm big enough to eat by myself," he announced.

"Of course, of course," murmured Plum Nelly, hiding a grin, "but even a good pump has to be primed sometimes. When you and Kit finish eatin', I got business to talk with you."

The boys felt better. What business could Plum Nelly have with them on the very day they were going home? Why would he wait until the last day? They could hardly wait to find out. Was it about the secret panel?

Sandy's appetite improved right away, and Kit put away the last of his pancakes with a flourish, even lifting his plate and pretending to lick the last drop of maple syrup. They carried their dishes to the sink and piled them neatly.

"You know," said Kit, raising his eyes to Plum Nelly's face, "we did feel pretty beat when we got up this morning." He hesitated. "I didn't think I could eat as much as Sandy here did."

"Somehow it tasted better after you said you wanted to talk business with us," Sandy added. He made "business" sound like a very, very important word. Plum Nelly caught on right away.

He motioned the boys back to the table. "This is important business," he said seriously, "most important. It's a good thing your father got up early for grouse. With him away, we men can discuss something I've had in mind fer a long spell. Yup," he went on, "fer quite a spell."

Kit's chest swelled. This must be important, and Plum Nelly had called him and Sandy "men." He kicked Sandy's foot so his brother would pay attention.

"Now then," Plum Nelly said briskly, "you men are in your teens—Kit here is a mite older than Sandy, but not enough to bother with. Why, I remember I was earnin' a livin' when I wuz your age. But that's neither here nor there. What I was wantin' ter say was this—"

Sandy, too impatient to let Plum Nelly finish, interrupted. "Yes, Plum Nelly, what were you going to say?"

"Great guns and pickled pigs' feet!" Plum Nelly roared, getting red in the face. "Can't you let me finish?"

"Yes, *sir*," answered the shame-faced Sandy. And Kit kicked him again.

"Well, as I was saying," Plum Nelly continued, "an' no interruptions, mind you—as I was saying, I reckon it's time you was goin' home—and ter school. Winter's comin' up here—there's white frost on the ground this morning—and before long snow will fall. And chimney smoke is goin' straight up. That's a sign, all right. Understand?" Without waiting for an answer, Plum Nelly pulled a little smooth stick from his pocket. He waved it back and forth.

It looked like any softwood stick: about four inches long, smooth, perfectly round. But one end tapered and the other came to a little ball the size of a marble. Kit reached to feel it.

"Whoa there!" Plum Nelly yanked it away. Kit's fingers closed on air. "Did I tell you to touch it?"

This time it was Kit who said, "No, *sir*."

Plum Nelly twirled the smooth, yellowish stick, making it go faster and faster, faster and faster, until it looked to the boys as if a dozen sticks were leaping and dancing and twirling. It leaped and spun in his hand. It jumped like a living thing. *Up and down, round and round, faster and faster, and up, round, and faster.*

Then a funny thing happened. Color seemed to spring from the twirling, spinning wand. Blues and reds and pinks and greens sparkled. Sandy thought he saw streaks of gold and silver. Kit just sat with his mouth open, eyes going every which way.

There didn't seem to be any Plum Nelly. There was just the dancing whirl of brilliant colors, blending and changing like a rainbow doing a fast polka. Out and out reached the hues, creeping across the table, across the floor, up the walls, until there weren't any walls. There was only a volcano of ever-changing, whirling crimson and turquoise and shimmering silver.

One minute the whole cabin blazed in color, and the next, quicker than one can say "rabbit-in-rabbit-out," there sat Plum Nelly calmly twirling a smooth little stick with a taper at one end and a ball at the other. There were no greens, no reds, no blues, no shimmering silver. The cabin walls stood sturdy and strong as always.

Sandy dug his eyes with a tight fist.

Kit's mouth still hung open.

More and more slowly danced the stick, until it clattered to the table and lay quiet.

"Understand?" said Plum Nelly, scooping up the wand and thrusting it deep in a pocket. "See what I mean now?"

But Sandy still blinked, and Kit only half closed his mouth.

"Can't say I blame you much fer not understandin'." Plum Nelly scraped his chair back and stood up, shaking himself as if he, too, were coming out of a half dream. "When you git your mouth closed up, Kit, I'll be back, but right now I got ter set this blamed pot on. Your father will be wantin' a cup of coffee when he comes in. Mornin' grouse hunting kin be mighty chilly this time of year, I know."

"Come on—" Sandy nudged Kit—"let's go, too. I want to ask him something."

"Plum Nelly," said Sandy in the kitchen, "could I do that too?"

"Do what?"

"You know what I mean."

"Haven't the faintest idea," answered Plum Nelly, peering into the coffee pot.

Sandy hesitated. This wasn't going to be easy, and Kit was no help. "Could I make . . . make colors with your stick?" Now that he had said it, he was scared that maybe he'd said too much.

"Don't know what you mean."

"Yes you do, Plum Nelly." Sandy just had to find out. "Could I make pretty colors with your little stick?" Kit still stood silent.

"Coffee will be just about right when your father comes home. Now then," said Plum Nelly briskly, "you aim ter know 'bout my stick, do yuh? You got your mouth shut yet, Kit?"

"It's closed," Kit said.

"Keep it that way an' I'll tell you a story—a tale of the medicine man's wand. Better get set, for although it's not a long story, it's an important one. Fetch my pipe, will you, Sandy? This rocker suits me fine—you perch on the bench."

"Now then," said Plum Nelly, pushing the blackened pipe into his tobacco pouch, "we're all comfortable and snug. And mind you, you lads keep quiet or there'll be no yarn of the medicine man's wand.

"A long time ago, 'bout this time of year, I was fretting about winter comin'. We were cuttin' logs for Rat Portage —that's up Canada ways—and the boss was worried about when snow would fall. The best logging is done in winter, you know, when there's snow on the ground. It's easier to sled logs out on snow than over bare ground. Anyways, the weather was cold enough, but there just wasn't any snow a-fallin'. Not enough to fill a snuff can.

"You know, a jack somehow jest don't feel right if snow don't come—naked ground, huts without white roofs, trees still green, and lots of noise. Snow blankets sound, making winter forests quiet and still and not loud and crackly like in summer. Some folks say that logging oxen are restless an' won't work right if snow don't come.

"Every evenin' and every mornin' our foreman sniffed the air fer snow, peering at the clouds and stampin' up and down when it didn't fall. It got so bad that the men's work fell off—they wuz more concerned with weather than with lumberin'. But when the cook got surly an' lost interest in serving tolerable grub, I knew right then something jest had to be done.

"The trouble was, I didn't know what ter do. One day Jacques Devaux was chopping. His ax slipped and cut deep into flesh an' bone because he had one eye on a cloud patch and not both eyes on what he was doin'. The boss sent me with him to town to be sewed up.

"Comin' home alone, I wuz trampin' the trail, thinkin' how nice everything would be it only it would snow and be a right an' proper winter, when I come upon this here Indian. An old feller, he was, a wizened-faced little fellow, sittin' half crouched by a dead pine an' lookin' about as woebegone as our lumberjacks.

"Well, to make a long story short—and you boys got packin' to do—him and me got to talkin' and finally he said he was a medicine man and his tribe had sent him off to make magic and bring down some honest-to-goodness snow. I snickered at this, thinkin' how funny it was for anybody to think this dried-up little redskin could make it snow when no snow had fallen fer months.

"I kinda felt sorry fer him. After I gave him some tobacco we got friendly-like an' I said if we wuz ever goin' to get logs to Rat Portage it'd have to snow. Then he told me his tribe was mighty short of meat an' they could track deer better over snow ground. This sort of powwow went on, and he finally asked me to come back the next morning.

"I had no idee of doin' it, I tell you, but next morning there I was, hunkered down over a little fire with him. He looked like he'd been up all night. From somewhere under his buckskins he slipped out this little piece of wood, round at one end and tapered at the other. He begins to twirl it, makin' it go faster and faster and up and down and around and around. Never said a word, but jest keep twirlin'. Then I don't see the stick—just colors flashin' and sparkin' and makin' lights. All kinds of colors—reds and oranges and purples. Had to rub my eyes, I did, they wuz so bright. All of a sudden he dropped the wand, it spun a leetle on the bare ground, and lay quiet. 'Snow him come now,' the medicine man said.

"I just laughed. 'Okay, old man, but I don't believe it.'

" 'Snow come,' he insisted, and he picked up the queer little stick and put it between my palms. 'You friend, you take,' he said, and melted off into the woods.

"So I stuck the thing in my pocket and hit the trail

for camp, thinkin' how nice it would be if it would snow. Do you know, I wasn't halfway home before skies darkened, it got colder, and flakes fell. It snowed for two days, and that season we had more snow than we'd had for years. The old boy was right. My little stick always tells me when it's going to snow."

"But Plum Nelly," Kit said, "it isn't snowing now."

"Look out the window." Plum Nelly pointed. White, lazy flakes filled the air.

Sandy's eyes bulged, and he pressed his stubby nose to the pane as if not really believing what he saw. "You don't believe your stick had anything to do with that, do you, Plum Nelly?"

"It's snowing, isn't it?" answered Plum Nelly, knocking out his pipe. "Better get to your packing now, boys, before your father— Here he comes now, an' there's Dingo."

"Packed yet?" asked Mr. Duncan, spreading four fat grouse on the table. "If this snow hadn't come up, I wouldn't have missed the last bird. Spoiled my aim, it did. Didn't think it would snow this morning, did you, Plum Nelly?"

"Eh?" stammered Plum Nelly, pouring coffee. "What? Oh, I reckoned it might. Never can tell in these parts this time of year." He changed the subject rapidly. "I'll clean the birds—you better pack. It's a long trip home." He started to pick up the grouse, then looked at the boys. "Guess you better explore behind the panel before you pack. That's the real business I was going to talk about. Be back in a minute."

But Kit and Sandy stood still, staring at the snow.

"Wake up! Get a move on!" Mr. Duncan hurried into the bunkroom. The boys heard him grunt out of boots and snap his gun apart.

"Guess we'd better open the panel," Kit whispered. "Dad won't like it if we're not ready when he is."

The combination clicked and the door swung open. This time the paper read: *Everything comes to those who wait.*

"But there's no clue," protested Sandy. "It doesn't say to do anything."

Kit looked disappointed. "It sure doesn't. I bet—"

Plum Nelly banged in, making so much noise that Yellow Dog Dingo, tired from hunting, growled at having his rest disturbed. "Mighty nice birds," Plum Nelly called to Mr. Duncan. "I'll wrap 'em for you to take home. Now, what in tarnation is the matter with you boys? You packed yet?"

Sandy held out the panel's paper. "What does this mean? It doesn't tell us to *do* anything," he complained.

"We can't wait," Kit added. "We're going home today."

"True enough," agreed Plum Nelly, "but if it says to wait, there's nothing to do but wait. Want a hand with your packing?"

Plum Nelly was a master packer. His quick hands folded and filled duffel bags with jackets, shirts, jeans, socks. He kept Sandy jumping to hand him boots and all kinds of this and that. Plum Nelly made Kit fold the blankets three time before he was satisfied. They took down the casting rods and put reels in cases. He made them wrap their wonderful new lures in paper and tied the box with brown paper and string. He told Sandy to take the old rifle and powder flask to the car. He was so full of orders and directions that Mr. Duncan finally said the boys would be worn out before they ever left. Plum Nelly packed Kit's cap and then scolded him because he came in with snow on his hair.

Eventually the job was done. "Great guns and pickled pigs' feet, I never saw so much truck," Plum Nelly complained. "You sure everything is in?"

"Sure," said Mr. Duncan. "I checked."

"Me too," added Kit.

And Sandy, not knowing what to say, said, "Me too!"

"Jest what I thought," exclaimed Plum Nelly disgustedly. "Jest what I thought!"

Mr. Duncan wheeled around. "You thought what? Do you mean we forgot something?" Plum Nelly nodded.

"Well, what?" Mr. Duncan was in a hurry.

"You forgot the waiting," said Plum Nelly calmly.

Sandy pulled Kit's sleeve. "If he starts another story, we'll never get home." Somehow, now that the car was loaded, Sandy was eager to start.

"Come on, boys, let's go." Mr. Duncan walked toward the door.

"Now, jest a minute—jest hold yer horses."

"But Plum Nelly—"

"You forgot the waiting," said Plum Nelly firmly, "and these boys aren't goin' till the—"

"Oh, golly," Kit exclaimed, "We forgot the last clue— you know, 'Everything comes to those who wait.' The secret panel's last secret."

"Now you're talkin'! That's my boy," said Plum Nelly. "That's the *big* business."

He flourished a birchbark roll. "Hear this! Hear this! Maybe you better read it, Sandy." He thrust the roll into Sandy's hand.

"Bro-*ther!*" said Sandy. "Will you look at this!"

His father and Kit saw a fancy document penned in ink. A red seal of wax decorated a bottom corner, and under the seal were blue ribbons. The writing said:

KNOW YE, *that Plum Nelly Jones of Broadwater Lodge in the Name and by the Authority of the North Woods and in Recognition of Their Good Behavior and Lessons in Woodcraft Does Hereby Appoint and Commission*

KIT AND SANDY DUNCAN

Backwoods Colonels and Orders Them to Spend Next Summer at Broadwater Lodge.

In Testimony Thereto, I have Set My Hand and Caused the Great Seal of the Agropelter to Be Affixed.

(*Signed*) PLUM NELLY JONES

"Do you mean it, Plum Nelly—do you *really* mean it?" Sandy gasped.

"You want us all summer?" Kit couldn't believe the good news.

"Great guns and pickled pigs' feet, of course I want you. And you're coming, aren't they?" He smiled at Mr. Duncan.

"If you want them, they'll be here," said the boys' father.

"Thanks, Plum Nelly. Gee, thanks a lot!" Kit's freckles stood plain as red kernels on a white corncob.

"Get along with you now, or you'll be late gettin' home." Plum Nelly shooed the lads into the car. Yellow

Dog Dingo, not understanding all the excitement, barked and danced around so that Sandy had to jump out and haul him in by the collar.

"Thanks for everything, Plum Nelly," grinned Mr. Duncan. The car jounced forward.

"So long, Plum Nelly," called the boys.

Plum Nelly's big voice followed them. "Good-by, colonels! See you next summer."

Then the falling white snow blotted him out.